CLA RLD

.Y 2025 - ISSUE 226

FICTION

NON-FICTION

Neil Clarke: Publisher/Editor-in-Chief
Sean Wallace: Editor
Kate Baker: Non-Fiction Editor/Podcast Director

Clarkesworld Magazine (ISSN: 1937-7843) • Issue 226 • July 2025

clarkesworldmagazine.com

Missing Helen

TIA TASHIRO

When Mark told you he was marrying your clone, you said "congratulations" on autopilot, because that's what you say when your friend tells you they're getting married, and you had promised to stay friendly after the divorce.

You studied his face, his fingers crimping the pleats of his dress pants. That judgmental twist crept onto the corner of your lips without you quite realizing it. Mark—poor Mark—was out of place in the living room you'd once shared. Sunk down into the ratty secondhand sofa you must've bought when, in a fit of pettiness, you'd thrown out the old one. Sitting there in his suit, his salt-and-pepper hair slicked back in the dashing way you used to like, he could tell you thought him as awkward as a child in grown-up clothes.

"It's all right if you need some time to process it," Mark said.

You leaned lazily back against the counter, giving him a terse smile. You were every inch Helen of Troy, his old nickname for you—imperious, lovely, beating your shock into submission. "That's okay," you said—then, lamely, "I thought you were going to ask for a kidney or something."

He saw the quick flicker of your gaze toward the end of a Band-aid sticking out from under his sleeve, covering up the tail of his reef shark tattoo. A crack in your uncaring façade. A glimpse into your psyche. Your matching one undulated up the inside of your wrist, an organic curve of stippled ink. You'd gotten them on your fifth anniversary, when he'd surprised you with a trip to Australia in an attempt to revitalize the sagging skin of your marriage.

You'd seen the shark that inspired the tats while on a guided scuba dive over a once-bleached expanse of the Great Barrier Reef. Advancements in marine regenerative tech had repopulated enough polyps that the coral was making a comeback, blooms of red and orange branching up through the water. Fish wove in and out of the recuperating ecosystem.

You both pushed a burst of air through your regulators when you saw the shark, its gray back rippling with sunlight as it swept through the ocean. You told him the shark was proof of concept that, as a species, you hadn't fucked it up as royally as you'd thought.

What a memory: The shark. The fish. The reef.

"Just like our marriage," he'd joked later in the cabana. "Coming back to life."

That's the kind of story you'd think his fiancée might be jealous of, though you wouldn't know he's already told her. Already bared your shared stories, your flaws, all to assuage her lingering doubts. He's an honest man; honesty is attractive. You must've known that, once.

The Band-aid is a reminder. He already has an appointment to remove the tattoo next week, long before the wedding.

You sold the rights for your cloning the week after you were legally emancipated, freshly sixteen and flat broke. Just like you had done your research for the emancipation—found the forms, collected the evidence of neglect and verbal abuse, submitted the appropriate documentation to the courts—you had already identified the best site to put your genetic material up for sale.

It was called Angels in Advance. Profiles of people marched past, all ages—flattering pictures. (Some were tagged with yellow warning banners that the site generated when it suspected AI airbrushing, its detection software picking up signs of augmentation imperceptible to the human eye. To avoid liability for misleading images, Angels in Advance made it clear its visitors were responsible for verifying the accuracy of posted pictures before completing a purchase.) The profiles were accompanied by college admissions test scores, zodiac signs, favorite breakfast foods—whatever miscellanea people thought would get their picture chosen by discerning (and, hopefully, rich) future parents.

There used to be sites like AIA for buying eggs or sperm. *This egg comes from a basketball star; this sperm is sourced from a Pulitzer finalist.* Those sites were still popular with some—but they were also a risk. You didn't know exactly what you were getting. The clay could fire in any form.

Angels in Advance gave you the pot, premade. You knew exactly what kind of kid you were getting.

Years later, when you were explaining all this to Mark, you told him it was your best shot. You knew you were pretty, on the good days when acne didn't prickle your hairline; you were moderately athletic (after-school sports practices kept you out of the house); and, most importantly, you were smart. Perfect scores on the precollege tests you'd taken, and you were barely a junior.

You uploaded your scores and polished your profile on the site long before you turned sixteen. You'd taken your picture on your best friend Ronit's phone against a blank school library wall, tucked among moldering editions of history textbooks and out-of-date science tomes. You captioned the photo simply, no last name as per Angels in Advance requirements: *Helen*. As soon as you aged into eligibility, you clicked the button to submit.

Your first offer came two days later.

You didn't take it, as much as your fingers itched for the cash. You only had one shot at this—legally speaking, you could sell the rights to yourself just once every two decades, an attempt to address concerns about overcloning and create generational distance. The offer was good, but you thought, if you left the profile up just a bit longer, you could do better. You were so sharp, even then, even young.

It was hard to wait. You were living in Ronit's house, and while you liked her parents, you couldn't shake the fear that they'd wake up one morning, decide they'd expended their stores of compassion for the foreseeable future, and shove you out the door.

Your third morning on the site, you woke up to three offers and an increased bid from the first couple. One of those offers, pending a brief interview, would put you through an associate's degree if Ronit's parents stayed kind, or get you a place to stay to ride out high school if they didn't.

You didn't press your luck. Just clicked *Accept* and signed yourself away.

Mark is the kind of man who laughs with abandon, who remembers the waiter's name and tips generously, who goes to therapy once a year like some people check the brakes on their cars: just to make sure the machinery's still running smoothly. He's clean-cut and organized. His parents are supportive. He's a catch.

You didn't know these things about him when he first moved to your city. You'd talked yourself out of the associate's degree before high school graduation, pragmatism trumping college dreams, and taken an apprenticeship as an electrician with a program specializing in bot tech. You were progressing well, nearing the end of your training. You liked unravelling tricky problems the best, diagnosing a malfunctioning bot like a doctor might a patient.

Kamal, one of your closest friends in the program, had an older sister who'd gone to college with Mark. When Mark moved to the area, that friend-of-a-friend connection was enough for him to end up as one of the few unfamiliar faces that sometimes cycled through your intermittent get-togethers. You barely noticed him at that first barbecue, one more forgettable laughing boy, his gaze light on yours as he offered to flip burgers.

But he noticed you. He watched you watching people, attentive, alert, interjecting with a well-timed joke or sardonic comment. You worked your way through the party like it was a test you could ace.

There were a few more events, ones you skipped or he did, where the skeins of your lives could've tangled but didn't. He got your number off Kamal and made first contact. Asked you out for drinks.

You showed up to the rooftop bar before he did, and when he caught your eye from across the space, you were wiping sweaty palms on the fabric of your floral dress. Poking out from beneath it was a thick black walking boot.

"Sorry I'm late. Parking," Mark said. He gestured to your cast. "Love the choice of footwear for the evening."

You forced a laugh, or he drew a genuine one out—maybe something in between. "Right? Accident with a bot. Ungrateful hunk of metal broke my foot."

"And here I thought you were just fashion forward."

You wiggled your toes from out the end of the boot. "Not the best impression for a first date?"

"On the contrary." Mark snagged a menu off an abandoned table. "I'm duly impressed by your toe mobility."

Your next laugh was unburdened. Fully real.

He'd liked you before then, but that laugh caught his heart and kept it. You, though. You'd been on a slew of first dates in your life. You'd calculated carefully the masks that would carry you untouched through each one. You knew better than to trust a smooth repartee, a dashing face. You were the kind of paradoxical woman who, yearning for love, built seawalls to keep it out.

But Mark was persistent. An ebb and flow of gentle affection, from your first date to the second, third, fourth, until you stopped counting. Until he'd eroded away those walls. Until you finally let him in.

When Mark asked you to marry him, three years after his slow slide into courtship, you sat down on the grass in the middle of the park and started to cry. You could barely snuffle through the tears into a *yes.*

"You have to promise," you finally got yourself to say, smiling, snot dribbling out of your nose. "You have to promise. This is it."

A joyful response, and the bitter aftertaste of your manipulation. You probably didn't mean it that way. You had been on your own for so long; it only makes sense that you'd cling to the first person to want you like you wanted them. A burr in a sock, a claw snagging fabric, a child refusing to let go. Still.

"Of course, baby," Mark said, so happy it was spilling out his edges. He took your bait; couldn't help it. He knelt next to you, knees crumpling the grass, and slipped the ring onto your finger, wiping your tears away. "Of course, I promise. That's why they call them vows, isn't it? This is it, Helen. 'Til death do us part."

Your wedding: A ceremony. Rings, vows, Kamal giving a speech. You loved Mark's parents almost as much as the thought of fitting neatly, seamlessly into their family, a family of your own. It helped ease the burn of an audience bereft of your own relatives.

Your wedding: A fete. Reception, dancing, a honeymoon suite. You didn't insist, but you gave him one of your *looks,* and he made the reservation without a thought to your budget. His parents' budget.

Mark didn't know what he was signing up for.

Your wedding: not worth lingering on.

You have always been a fanatic for the details—your nature, not nurture. When you and Mark were first dating, you prodded him for the intricacies of his relationships before you. He'd had a few, one stretching for a year before the boyfriend had a crisis and left polite society to join a zero-carbon commune.

You wheedled your way into descriptions of his first dates: those aborted starts, late-night conversations, the ways his exes had acted around him. Perhaps you wanted to see what had caused those potential futures to fizzle; more likely, you wanted him to calm your fears, pick at the facets and failures of those people for you, prove that they'd never been meant for him.

Perhaps it's unkind to say that you were insecure or therapizing to presume it was the dregs of your childhood tainting the taste of new love. But you'd admit it to yourself. You were fiercely independent in every other part of your life, from your finances to the bots to the aikido you'd picked up when you were nineteen.

Mark was the only one who'd earned your reliance. He'd been admitted into your inner sanctum. Your vulnerability was a gift.

Cute in the early days. Just a part of the relationship during the engagement, the wedding, something he had come to accept: constant messages, calls, reassurances. Your anxiety bled through the marriage.

And slowly, slowly, it began to grate.

Mark—so kind, so open, so willing to learn—realized that he did not understand you.

It came slowly, like the love had to you. He worked in ad targeting—he liked to think he could tell what would reach a person, *any* person. But your small traumas, those he had long learned to work around and those that would arise unexpectedly, created a minefield of a marriage. He hadn't minded, once, when he hadn't yet become accustomed to your intelligence, to your flashes of laughter. When they hadn't lost their shine.

Mark, who never worried what he'd do if there was suddenly no roof over his head. Mark, whose parents showered him with love, a net beneath the tightrope of his career if ever he should fall. Mark, who never had to sell his genome for the price of a better life.

The blame for the failure of your marriage can be shared. It was Mark who drew back, didn't bring up habits of yours that had begun to chafe. He threw money and time at the problem instead of words, lavish vacations and long weekends paired with meaningless chatter.

Once or twice—maybe more—you asked him if something was wrong.

"It feels like . . . " You picked at the wilting salad on your plate, pushing a few dreary leaves to the side—or possibly it was salmon, your favorite, already half-eaten. "Like we're just *missing* each other, somehow. Not on the same page. Do you feel that?"

"No," Mark said on instinct—and then, it would've been awkward to retract such a denial. He munched down on his burger instead. Too greasy, melted American cheese dripping morosely off the edges. He chewed, thinking of all the ways he could tell you things needed to change, but when he swallowed, what came out instead was: "Nothing's wrong, Helen. Let's get a takeout box. We're going to miss the tour bus."

These were difficult topics to broach. Forgive him; he didn't know how.

You'd think you'd have wondered about your clone more often.

You didn't. You knew, vaguely, that she was somewhere out there in the city—a big enough city that Angels in Advance didn't exclude intracity matches. AIA had a strict no-contact policy, part of the extensive legal document you'd signed when you accepted your offer. A clone might reach out to their genetic donor once they reached the age of majority, but the reverse was strictly prohibited.

You didn't care. Those sold stem cells were faint in your memory, your clone an exercise in the abstract. You'd needed money. The clone had been a way—much less invasive than donating half your liver or going to the plasma banks every few weekends—to procure it.

Somewhere in the city was another you, a different you, a younger you, but you knew your lives would never overlap.

Mark expected you to cry when he served you the divorce papers, or to ask him to wait just a little longer, or to beg him to reconsider.

Instead, you paged through the paperwork on your tablet with hands as sure and callused as one might expect from a master electrician. You allowed the tablet camera to scan your face, verifying your identity, as you reached the end of the document.

"Helen—" he said, but you just clicked *Accept* and signed your marriage away.

You turned to him. Your eyes were glistening, enough to notice, but that was the only sign it affected you. "It's okay, Mark," you said. "I think we both knew this was coming." You spun your wedding ring with your thumb, the way you always did when you lied, then caught yourself. You pulled it off and set it gently on the tablet screen, on the counter.

(It's a beautiful ring—his great-grandmother's, pricked with authentic mined diamonds. Two delicate sapphires buttressing the larger gems. Gold. A perfect fit.)

"I'm sorry." He scratched at the nape of his neck, made suddenly awkward by your compliance. "I . . . look, you . . . "

"You don't have to explain." You smiled, a shield. "Let's be cordial, if we can?"

"I'd like to stay friends," he said, tentatively. "I'll miss you."

"Sure, sure."

He could tell. Something had snapped; something had shifted.

You had your inner sanctum, and he was no longer a part of it.

It was about six months later that he downloaded one of those cheesy personality-match dating apps. He filled out the adaptive questionnaire and waited until the AI engine had sorted through all the other app users. It spat out a selection of ten profiles for his perusal.

He stared at profile number six, a sense of déjà vu washing over him. The woman in the picture was smiling, mouth open, one arm flung around a cropped-out friend. He could hear her laugh.

The picture read *Elaine.* The app informed him that they were ninety-seven percent compatible.

He reached out, expecting nothing. At first, he was going to bring up the coincidence—something to laugh about, a crazy story to tell. He wasn't really thinking of another relationship. He didn't want another you.

It's just that, once he'd messaged the woman on the app, once they met, once he knew exactly what to say to spark chemistry between them . . .

Your ex-husband changed his mind.

Your clone is an adult, a recent graduate, doing very well for herself. After Mark told you about the engagement, you must've felt the wounds of that old relationship fresh again. He has moved on; you have not. You must've pulled out a tablet and searched up his social media, found her tagged, followed the breadcrumbs to her accounts. You must've found pictures of her partying with friends, pressing a kiss to his cheek, working from a favorite café for the remote internship she snagged fresh out of college.

Oh, Helen, you must've done all this, because you show up to that café two weeks later, the laurel of silver bells on the door handle jingling as you push it open, and I see you before you see me.

I freeze, my laptop flipped open in front of me to one of the boring articles all the interns have to edit before they let us get to the good stuff. You lift your chin to the smell of coffee, brushing back a strand of hair. I've seen pictures, some low-key cyberstalking of my own once Mark told me about you, but it's nothing compared to you in person.

I'm not you. Am you. Your clone, your shadow, your genetic echo. You are me in another life. We are each other's alternate universe.

You turn away from the door, late-spring rain beading your hair, and catch my eye.

The differences between us span sixteen years, but I can summarize them in a few words. Crow's feet at the corners of your eyes. Lipstick, pixie cut, outfit, all as severe and unassailable as your bearing. Sharp eyes, intelligent eyes, *my* eyes. *Helen of Troy*, I think, Mark's nickname for you coming easily.

I swallow, reminding myself of all the flaws we don't share: your insecurity, your trauma, your age. I am the best of you, and I straighten as you approach, laying my hand on the café table so the ring is clearly visible. Diamonds, sapphires, gold. A perfect fit.

I expect an attack.

Instead, you smile. There's a gap between your front teeth—one I used to have, before middle school braces took care of it. "Hi," you say. "Elaine? Mind if I sit down?"

I gesture toward the empty chair at the other side of my table, keeping my laptop up. "Please." I don't like the way you carry yourself, that easy confidence. It wars with the way Mark has described you, the twitches in your countenance, fault lines of your flaws.

"You're betrothed to Mark Brandt, is that right? It's nice to meet you. I'm Helen. Though I think you already knew that."

"Mark told me."

"I thought he might've." You lean back, crossing your legs. "He would've told me, if I'd asked. And of course I would've asked."

A few words, laying me bare. *Of course I would've asked*, mirroring the way that I did, that I have. All those late nights with Mark, when I pushed to know more about you—the two of you. Even those questions that salted my own jealous wounds: your first date, your wedding, your honeymoon. I still asked, and Mark answered. Some details supplied by him, others by my imagination, coalescing to shape your story.

I know every intricacy of you.

"You're not allowed to contact me," I say. "I'm your—" *clone* cloys in my mouth.

"You're certainly old enough," you say. "And as far as I'm aware, this is a strange coincidence. I haven't messaged you or harassed you." You shrug. "I'm just . . . here. I want to talk. Is that so bad?"

"You want to talk about Mark."

"No," you say, "I want to talk about *you*. Elaine." You rummage in your purse for a moment and pull out two flavored chocolates wrapped in green foil—my favorite kind of mint. You offer me one.

"No thanks. I don't take candy from strangers."

You unwrap both and pop them in your mouth. "I never forgot you, you know. I thought about you all the time. Wondered where you were, what you were doing. Who you were becoming."

"I don't believe you." I should've known you'd start this conversation off with a lie. "Mark told me you never brought me up. Not once, except at the very beginning, when you told him I existed."

"I didn't tell Mark everything I thought, all of the time." You crinkle up the candy foil into a glinting ball and set it on the table. "It was a sensitive subject, for me. I didn't have another choice when I sold my . . . when I sold the rights to AIA. But knowing you were somewhere out there felt like . . . like a book I'd begun but never finished. A loose thread." Your gaze darts up to mine, and for the first time, I see hesitation in it. Concern. "I never dreamed he'd reach out to you."

I have a moment, there in the café, sitting across from a version of myself in sixteen years, where certainty coalesces.

Without quite realizing it, I've been mirroring your body language. Picking up the cues in the rhythm of your breathing, the movement of your fingers, the way you offered me the mints and the way you ate them yourself. Our lives, our experiences, may have split us in twain, but I can read you as easily as myself.

You are telling the truth.

I close my laptop.

"I thought about you, too." My hands, on the table, are quivering, just slightly. I still them. "You're not on any of the socials. I looked."

"No, I'm not. I . . . the situation with my biological parents was complicated. That was one of the reasons I wondered. I wanted to know if you were—"

"Loved?" we say, a harmony of two.

I draw my coffee mug toward me and wrap my hands around it, even though it's empty—to steady myself, I suppose. I'm embarrassed, for a moment, at the untidiness of my small café table; a few napkins lie haphazardly strewn by half a lox bagel, uneaten on its plate. I reach out and straighten them with one hand. "I'm sorry." I laugh—you can probably tell it's fake. "It's not fair, I guess. You not knowing me. Me knowing you."

"You knowing *about* me," you correct. *Through Mark* lingers unsaid.

"Is there a difference?"

"Hmm." You reach out and tap the edge of my plate, indicating the lox bagel. "Salmon?"

"Yeah," I say, emboldened. "Our favorite."

You crinkle your nose, the way I do when I'm about to contradict someone. "*Your* favorite, maybe. I got food poisoning from expired salmon once. Put me off it ever since." You give the plate a little push toward me and lean back. "You're right, though, that I don't know you at all. I never even met your parents in person—we just had a short video call through AIA."

"Well, my mom and dad are still together," I say. "They didn't talk about you at all when I was growing up. But that's not weird. I have an older brother, also from AIA, and they paid the same for his genetics as mine because they didn't want either of us to feel different. More or less wanted. Anyways, they didn't tell him anything, either. About his . . . um . . . original." The corner of your mouth twitches up.

"I don't blame them," I hasten to add. "They just wanted us to know they considered themselves our parents, full stop. And yeah, to answer your question, I was loved. I *am* loved."

"Good," you say, smiling. A real smile. "I'm glad."

I don't know if I should tell you more. About how Mom and Dad fell in love at the tennis court and still go out and play sometimes, even though he's having trouble with his hip and her knees aren't what they used to be. How my older brother David is in law school, and I'm trying to make it as a journalist, and my dad doesn't get it, but he still buys me annual magazine subscriptions for my birthday. How my mom reads my freelance articles and brainstorms with me when I'm feeling stuck.

Did you want this for me? Any of it?

I fiddle with the corner of a napkin. "I don't . . . I'm sorry. If this isn't what you want to hear." You're probably comparing your family to mine even now. I'm probably opening old wounds.

"No," you say, sweeping out a hand—an inviting gesture. "Please. Tell me who you are, Elaine."

"Oh. Um. Okay." My breath flutters in my chest. For some reason, I feel the need to impress you. "I don't know where to start. One of my friends likes to do wallet tours, where you share stories about all the stuff in your purse or your wallet—a way to get to know someone. Or, I mean, I could tell you about my scars." I point to the thin line where my hair parts differently, the ghost of an old injury weaving from my temple along my scalp. "I got this one when I was six, from falling down the stairs. Busted my head open. Bled a ton. Mom rode with me in the ambulance."

You cock your head, listening, absorbing. I hurtle onward. I'm trying not to think, just letting myself spill out.

"Or I could talk about tennis. It was a huge part of my life for a long time—I played tennis just like my parents in high school, placed second in state my junior year, kept going through college until I strained my LCL on senior night. I did all that and kept my grades up, too, though you could've guessed that. We're both sharp, aren't we, Helen? I'd say I get that from you, but maybe we both get it from your parents—your bio parents, that is." I almost expect this to be a misstep, but your expression doesn't change. Are your distant parents now a distant era of your life?

I realize I'm trying to work my way to the point—the person—that links us. You and me. So next: "Or I could tell you about my exes. My first crush in high school—I was her witness in Mock Trial. It was an unrequited thing. She was nice about it, and eventually the feelings faded. And then the guy I dated from junior year until we left for college, and we tried long-distance for the first semester, but it petered out." That ex had written a breakup song about me—he'd called the end of our relationship "*The last sputter of charge in a dead battery.*" I hated that the lyric was kind of accurate. "Anyways, it was flings for a long time until Mark."

Your expression catches on hurt, despite how quickly you try to hide it, and I hold fast to my course of honesty. I feel like I'm running downhill, too much momentum to stop. "And at first, Helen, with Mark, I thought he was a loser. My friends did, too. He's old for me. I know that. But he was . . . charming, on the app, and I let him talk me into a date. There was chemistry. You'd know.

"I was still going to ghost him, until he messaged that he had a confession to make. And he told me about you."

I look down at my laptop and swallow, smoothing a hand over its silver surface. "I've never said this part out loud before. But . . . I didn't say yes to seeing him again because of him. I said it because of you. I . . . wanted to know. And the more he told me, the more I learned about you, the more I got it. Why he loved you. Why he could love me."

"You're the better version," you say, soft. "You're me without baggage."

"We all have baggage," I say. "I think he's just more comfortable with mine."

You laugh at that, surprising both of us—and, after a moment, I laugh alongside you. Twin voices, interwoven.

"I imagined this moment," I admit. "Meeting you. It's why I never reached out. I thought . . . I thought it'd be like a dog looking at its reflection. That we'd be too similar, and it would scare me, and I'd spend the whole time barking at you, and you'd never forgive me."

You smile, crow's feet at the corners of your eyes crinkling. "Are you done barking?"

You are a mystery resolved. Mists dispersing. You're not some mythical figure, imposing your will on my destiny. If you ever had that power, it was only insofar as I gave it to you. *Helen of Troy*, looming large in my imagination. An image bolstered by Mark—undercut by him, too, as he magnified the ways you fell short.

The small, comfortable noises of the café eddy around us. You run a hand through your hair, tucking a stray strand behind your ear—not one of my mannerisms, like some of your others. *Helen*, I think, trying to recategorize you in my head—to overlay this version of you atop Mark's. You're similar enough to understand me; different enough to be your own self, and leave me mine.

"I'm done barking," I say. "I . . . I have a lot to think about. But thank you. For coming, I mean. And listening."

You reach out to lay your hand across mine. A strange mirroring, the first time we've touched. Your palm is callused just like I imagined, and your skin is more wrinkled than mine, but the size, the shape of the fingers, the nails? A perfect match.

Our eyes meet. "Thank *you*, Elaine," you say, and you squeeze my hand once, lightly, before drawing back. Do I imagine it, or do you hesitate before letting go? "It was good to hear your story."

In the weeks after meeting you, I notice a change.

I start leaving Mark's messages unread for hours, then days. I shirk wedding planning. I dodge his affections, ducking under his chin when he tries to kiss me. I don't know how to tell him it doesn't feel right anymore; that whatever was between us has dissolved like cotton candy on my tongue.

He doesn't confront me. I knew he wouldn't—after all, it took him years to work himself up to the divorce—so it's up to me to ask him to meet me at Giovanni's. A public place, a restaurant with no memories of first dates or proposals: neutral ground.

"I'm sorry, Mark," I say at the end of the meal, and I give him back his great-grandmother's ring. Diamonds, sapphires, gold. It's started to feel a little tight.

"Elaine—"

"It's okay, Mark," I say. "I think we both knew this was coming."

I haven't talked to you since the café. But I think I get it now. Mark—charming, honest, handsome Mark—was my connection to you. I convinced myself it was more than that. As long as you were an enigma, I was drawn to Mark and his stories of you. As if I could know myself through them, get a glimpse at my own potential downfall, my strengths, my joys. A spell wound up in the mantra: *Helen of Troy*.

Meeting you broke that spell.

This story isn't about Mark.

It never was.

Here's how I picture it, Helen:

You're working hard on a bot when your tablet chimes. You get to your feet, wincing—your back is starting to ache. You really should stretch more. You lift the tablet and look down at a message routed through the Angels in Advance contact service.

Your clone is inviting you to connect! It's an official invitation; just by offering, I've freed you from your last contractual obligations to AIA. You can accept or deny my request—even block me. You don't have to say yes. Maybe you sated your curiosity when you confirmed for yourself that I had a good childhood, have a good family.

In making first contact, I've offered not an olive branch—there is no enmity between us—but an open hand.

I've been wondering if there's another reason you thought about me in the years since the donation. If you tried to convince yourself not to hope for me to reach out, because alongside that hope would come another. For a long time, my existence was the closest thing to family you had in the world.

I don't think you'd put that onto me. You wouldn't expect that the bonds between us mean more than double helices and your face reflected in mine. But what happened in that café left the door open to curiosity. To possibility.

Here's how I picture it, Helen: Your finger hovers over your tablet. You shift on your feet; your old broken bone twinges. You make your choice.

You click *Deny*, and that's it. You have your closure. I become a story for Ronit or Kamal or whatever other friends of yours Mark never told me about.

Or you click *Accept*, one more time, and sign yourself up for some kind of beginning.

ABOUT THE AUTHOR

Tia Tashiro is a multiracial science fiction and fantasy writer hailing from the Pacific Northwest. By day, she works in a neurobiology lab; by night, she writes; and in between, she dabbles in stained glass and juggling, though never at the same time. She is an Astounding Award finalist with short fiction published in *Clarkesworld, Uncanny,* and *Apex.*

The Walled Garden

FIONA MOORE

Not long after the local billionaire was shot by his own robots in the Georgian manor house he'd refitted as his survival bunker, Morag packed up her rucksack, left her parents' farm, and went out into the mountains to live as a nomad.

The villagers whispered that Morag, who had been working as a security guard at the manor at the time, had been the one to set the robots free from their programming restraints. She certainly was one of the few who had the skills, and it would explain why she'd been so haunted and silent when she came down from the Big House, the Big Man's two children hanging off her hands and crying.

And people whispered it a lot.

Meaning, it didn't surprise anybody when she walked out the farm gates with her rucksack, a sleeping bag, a slingshot, a utilitool, a tinderbox, and her father's copy of the *SAS Survival Guide*. Leaving behind her parents and the Big Man's children, now increasingly regarded as village children, and being known by their proper names of Zeb and Casey. Also leaving behind her phone, and her watch, and her tablet, and her headphones, and her little bundle of tiny picks and tweezers for fixing things.

Morag didn't think she'd want to touch anything technical ever again.

Twenty-five or thirty years later, Morag sat back on her heels in the mud of what had once been her parents' farm and said to her robot, "Well, that's the polytunnel done for, then, Seamus."

Seamus was occupied with digging a rectangular hole about the size and shape of its own body, using the aluminum claws on its front set of limbs and bracing itself on the other four.

Morag contemplated the rip in the polythene sheet, flapping in the cool early spring wind. Maybe it had been torn by a foraging animal, or maybe it had just given out on its own.

"I don't know where I'm going to get another," she said, "and I expect even if I could find one, it'd be expensive as hell. But the plastic-fixer in Pen-y-Groes has patched and patched and patched this one, and there's no real point in patching it anymore. It's got too many holes in it to keep the heat in now. So what do I do? Give up growing fruit?"

That was a very worrying idea. She was dependent on the fruits and vegetables she grew for vitamins; they made the regular diet less boring; and she sold any surplus to town-dwellers fresh or as preserves, meaning an income for her and better health for them.

"Ask Owen next door if I can use his?" Owen's polytunnels were in as bad a shape as hers, and the same was true of everyone else in the village who still used them. A lot of people were facing exactly the same problem as her.

Seamus finished digging its hole. Morag went over to look. Seamus had been doing that a lot lately, and, unlike most of Seamus' activities, there seemed to be no obvious practical reason. Most of the things it did—patrolling, carrying small objects on its back, warning her of danger, intervening in threatening situations—were exactly what you'd expect from something like Seamus. A repurposed security walkbot that had wandered away from the Big House after the massacre, and eventually found its way, decades later, to the spoil heap behind the village, and from there to Morag's farm.

Morag revised that mentally. It was a self-repurposed walkbot. She'd taught it some new routines and tricks since it had come to live with her, but it had joined her of its own accord, for its own reasons. And who knew what it had done for the many years it had presumably spent wandering the hills in between.

She supposed she could excuse it a few quirks and eccentricities.

A vague memory surfaced, involving other robots digging holes for no obvious reason. Another data point, but nothing that was helping her fix the polytunnels.

"So," she asked again, looking at the polytunnel, "what should I do?"

Morag's parents had been worried about her when she left, of course, but only in the way parents always worry about children. There was nothing terribly unusual about people going off to be nomads. The young got fed up with living on farms or in craft households. The old wanted a little excitement while they still had the energy for it. The traumatized wanted a new start. Sometimes the nontraumatized did too.

Mostly, they would join one of the more organized preexisting local nomadic tribes, like the Children of Flame or the Hawk Winds. But that wasn't Morag's way, and, after three years working in a squad of security guards with all the toxic hierarchies that sort of job acquires, she was distinctly wary of anything involving groups.

That was one of the things she really liked about being a nomad. She could go for days without seeing a single other human being, and, when she did see one, they generally left her alone.

Living off the land was easier than she thought. Even without her tech. Especially without her tech. Having been raised on an organic farm, and having spent a lot of time reading books on things like edible mushrooms and how to fish, keeping fed wasn't much of a problem. Keeping dry was harder, but she'd learned a few tricks, mostly involving pine boughs, that turned out to work well in practice. The tinderbox had an arrangement of mirrors, concentrating heat onto the tinder, so she didn't have to worry about keeping matches or sticks dry. The only large predators in those parts were the wolves, which had probably escaped from the environmental research facility out near Bangor that no one had heard from in a while. And the wolves usually left people alone, preferring easier meals.

And if she sometimes woke up from nightmares about the security robots silently and methodically gunning down the people who had once called themselves their masters . . . well, she could look out at the green hills and the sheep and the birds and it all seemed like something out of a novel.

She didn't think she'd ever want to go back to the village.

"What did people do before there was plastic?" she asked Naomi, who ran the post office and had a lot of time to read books, and so was a useful person to go to with questions like that.

Naomi frowned over her tea mug. Outside her small cottage next to the post office, Morag could see the lake, the dark green woods, and beyond that, the mountains, the sheep grazing on them like white flecks of snow. "Glasshouses, I think," she said, taking another scone. "Panels of clear glass, in wooden or lead frames."

"I suppose Nancy, the glazier in Portmeirion, might be able to make those? Wouldn't be cheap, though. And it'd take a long time."

"Back in the day, it was only rich people could afford them," Naomi agreed. "There was a while when they were cheaper, but that was down to industrialization."

"Which we don't have, and couldn't bring back even if we wanted to," Morag said, splitting a scone and covering it with butter. "What did people do before that? Die of malnutrition?"

Naomi shook her head. "Walled gardens."

"I'm assuming you don't mean in the Internet sense," Morag smiled slightly. Naomi was a little younger than her and still remembered the Internet and its language.

"Yes, and no," Naomi said. "People built gardens, within walls like the name implies, and yes, it was partly to keep people out. But the design helped maximize heat. Kept the garden warmer than it would have been. Before glass and polytunnels. There must have been one at the Big House. Did you see it, when you were up there?"

"I might have done." Morag vaguely remembered a set of crumbling, thick brick walls out behind the main manor building. Remembered the aluminum dome over them, like a planetarium, the interior painted with a blue sky with impossible fluffy clouds. "I think the Big Man turned it into a swimming pool and sauna. He wasn't interested in learning from history, really, except the bits about feudal lords with armies and control over lots of serfs."

She put up her own mental brick walls about that bit. The idea of being part of that army, of being someone who had to go and frighten and hurt and maybe kill the people she'd grown up with, to make sure they regarded him as their lord, was what had made her finally decide things couldn't go on as they were.

"I could go up there and look at it. See if it could be fixed."

"And if it can't, maybe we could still learn something from looking at how it's built," Naomi said. Abruptly, she looked tired.

"You okay?"

"Yes, yes, I'm fine. Just . . . the incomers." She didn't need to say much more. After the Big House fell, a few people had tried to do what the Big Man had wanted, and tried setting up feudal communities. With more success than the Big Man, but even then, eventually, they always went too far.

There'd been one group of feudalists nearby, a couple of years earlier, which had made some fairly significant territorial gains before it collapsed. Their final mistake had been trying to establish a presence in the area around Pen-y-Groes. The local nomads had banded together with Morag, Naomi, and the other villagers to let him know what they thought of hierarchies.

The problem was that when the feudalist group collapsed, it had left a not-insignificant number of soldiers and laborers without work and homes. And there were more and more people coming west out of the big cities, looking for someplace healthier to be. The tribes had absorbed a lot of people, but not everyone was cut out for nomadic life.

Some of the farmers had been happy to take on boarders in exchange for work, and Zeb and his husband Dai the Brewer had added a few more children to their huge extended family of strays and orphans, but within the village, it was becoming hard to find the room. And people were starting to make the sort of generalizing remarks about newcomers that usually led to trouble later on.

"All the more reason to build the garden," Morag said. "We need to house them, but we need to feed them as well."

"Then let's do this," Naomi said.

Three weeks into her life as a nomad, Morag woke up to see the robots.

Four or five of them. Security robots, probably from the Big House or from some other failed project, like the environmental research facility. White, six-legged oblongs, about the size of a collie dog, with an extendible arm on the anterior face.

Morag kept still and breathed quietly, like she would if they were wolves or deer. She realized she was being silly. It wasn't like she was going to frighten them off. Then she remembered that some of the robots had guns, and, if the guns didn't work, they were capable of killing with the retractable climbing claws on their legs alone.

She'd seen it happen. Was still seeing it happen, in front of her eyes, sometimes, when she hadn't put up her mental brick walls.

But these robots didn't seem interested in her. They were doing something a little way uphill, something that was interesting them.

Morag told herself not to anthropomorphize. But she remained still nonetheless, until they'd finished what they were doing and ambled on, back into the pine woods.

When she was sure they were gone, Morag clambered as quietly as she could out of her sleeping bag, off the bed of pine boughs she'd made to keep herself dry and comfortable, and went to look at what they'd been doing.

They'd been digging holes. Not randomly. In patterns. Geometrical shapes, stars and triangles and scraped traceries of dirt that looked oddly like mandalas.

Morag wondered why. It didn't seem to have any purpose. A random error? A routine that had once been useful, gone wrong? Something else—she remembered Zeb and Casey teaching a security robot how to do a haka, and had a giddy vision of robots dancing under the moon.

But she didn't really want to think about robots just then. She gathered her things and set out across the mountain.

• • •

"Well, here goes nothing," Morag said to Seamus. They were standing in front of the walled garden that used to be a swimming pool. The white aluminum dome of the roof was caved in, like a giant had stepped on it. The doors were solid, but the lock had been electronic, and it didn't take Morag more than a few minutes to break it.

She walked, silent, around the edges of the building. Looking at the pool, now a stained and cracked dip with a thick mat of algae growing over the water in the middle. Masses of rotten timbers that, when pushed aside, exposed a heating mechanism. "The sauna," Morag said aloud. Shafts of sunlight through the broken dome, illuminating heaps of rubbish, colonizing plants. Young pine trees and spreads of buddleia.

But the walls were still standing, and the geometry worked.

She could see the walled garden underlying the tiles and plastic. Like they were just a bad episode in its past, already fading away as the building itself endured.

Walking back out into the sunlight, she stopped and glanced over at the Big House. Parts of it were in ruins, thanks to decades of neglect. The leader of the collapsed feudal community had holed up in the East Wing cellars for a while after being beaten by the locals, until Morag had persuaded him to move on.

But she wasn't ready to go in there again herself.

She turned her back.

Morag had taken the digging, mandala-making robots as an omen, and it turned out to be a bad one. The day turned from overcast to drizzly to rainy, and Morag's foraging didn't turn out much, bar a few edible mushrooms and a couple of old motherboards.

Suddenly, a river of asphalt spread out before her, and she realized she was only a short walk from Porthmadog.

Morag got out the motherboards, looked at them critically. Suppressing the wave of memory of fixing the tech at the Big House. Of surreptitiously reprogramming the robots to allow them the choice, whether to keep working for the Big Man or not. Of what followed.

She concentrated on the motherboards, on the here-and-now. They were clean and in good condition, and could be repurposed or, if not, the metal could be harvested. The tech workshop in Porthmadog would probably trade her some credit with the grocery store. She strode into town and emerged an hour later much more cheerful, her bargaining skills with both the tech fixer and the grocer having gained her a loaf of bread, a wheel of cheese, and a jar of set honey.

By the time she reached the forest, the sun was on the horizon. She made herself a sleeping platform and a rain shelter out of pine branches, had a supper of bread, cheese, mushrooms, and honey, wrapped the leftovers carefully in the cloth bag the grocer had given her, and settled down to sleep.

She was wakened in the night by growls and scuffles.

Although she got out of her sleeping bag quickly enough, the wolf was faster, and the last she saw of her hard-won food was a flash of a gray tail as the scavenger raced into the pines.

"I know I'm not the only one who's running out of polythene sheets," Morag said to the assembled villagers in the Stag's Head. "And those of you who are doing okay for them, great, but when they run out, there won't be any more. And I've got an idea."

She passed round the book Naomi had found, with the marks in where the bits were about walled gardens.

"I've checked. The one up at the Big House can be fixed up. It'll take time and effort, but planting's done, and we can spare the time. Work shifts. We could pool our resources, and then all take shares in the garden."

"Would we appoint a full-time gardener?" Owen asked.

"We could do," Morag said; she'd thought of that as well. "But it might be more practical just for everyone to do their own gardening in it, and watch out for each other, like we do with the sheep grazing and other common land activities." Appointing a gardener also had its own dangers, leading to ideas about gatekeeping and control, and some people being worth more than others. The walled garden's walls had to be physical, not metaphorical.

There were a few general affirmative noises from the villagers.

"Unless someone else wants to, I'm happy to do the research and draw up plans." The response to this was definitely affirmative.

"When we know what we need, we can draw up a work rota. Allocate tasks based on skills and time." Naomi looked 'round the room.

"I'll go up to the archive at Portmeirion tomorrow," Morag said. "I'll catch a lift on Zeb's wagon when he delivers the beer to the inn and stay with Nancy the glazier. If any place will have materials on how to do this, it's there."

"It's about time someone did something about the Big House," Ellie, who ran the Stag's Head with her family, said. "It's not right, letting it go into ruin. We need to do something with it. Make it useful."

Morag suppressed a surge of complicated emotion. "Yeah," she said. "Let's get that walled garden going first, though, eh?"

• • •

Morag walked to the coast the next day to fish, which gave her plenty of contemplation time for figuring out the food storage problem. Clearly, she needed to find a way to keep surplus food, particularly attractive surplus food like bread and cheese, out of the jaws of wolves and other scavengers. She still had the honey, but that was only because they hadn't managed to break the jar.

Some kind of bag, she thought, giving up on the fish and packing up her line. A bag and a rope. Something she could haul into the trees. Wolves can't jump or climb. Foxes can, but they're not likely to go to that much trouble.

But what could she make the bag out of?

She managed to bring down a hare with a slingshot later that afternoon and skinned it with more care than usual. Perhaps she could collect enough animal skins to stitch together into a storage bag.

But she had no idea how to preserve skins, and by the next day, the hare skin was beginning to make a nauseating smell and attract flies. She left it for the scavengers and went back to thinking her way around the problem.

"I'm afraid this is all we've got," Saiorse said apologetically.

Morag frowned at the collection assembled on the melamine desk in one of Portmeirion's study rooms. "A couple of books, one of them a fantasy novel, and four back issues of *Town and Country* magazine."

"We did have more, but they were too badly damaged in the floods ten years ago to save." Saoirse winced. "And I suppose people didn't think writing that sort of thing down was important enough. I'm afraid you've had a wasted journey. It's a good fantasy novel, though? Written by a local author."

"Preservation's so random," Morag smiled to show she wasn't upset. "We'll just have to start from first principles. Shame none of the professors who started this place was an architect, eh?"

"Actually, we did have one." Saoirse frowned speculatively. "Robert Novack. But he hasn't been around for a good fifteen years. He turned nomad."

"So . . . " Morag said, "he would have joined The Unmutuals?"

"Yes." The Unmutuals' territory was mostly in the hills around Portmeirion. That was the way things were becoming, Morag reflected. Most little towns had a band of nomads walking a circuit around the area. Villagers who got itchy feet joined the nomads. Nomads who got tired or sick came back to the towns. Both of them loved and hated the land, and each other, in different ways and from different perspectives.

"But he wouldn't have cracked a book in all that time, even assuming he's still alive."

"Doesn't matter. People have great memories."

"Without writing?"

"Especially without writing. Do you know where The Unmutuals are camped?" Morag pulled on her jacket. "Come on, let's go find them. Seamus?"

The little robot usually settled down in power-saving mode in a corner of the room when it didn't have anything else to do, like a dog taking a nap. But it wasn't there.

After a bit of searching, they found it in a room with a lot of optical equipment. It had arranged pieces of colored glass and domed lenses on the floor in a careful pattern, pushing them with its forelimbs.

"Seamus! I'll have to clear that up, and I've no idea where it all goes!" Saoirse exclaimed, her plump cheeks going pink with emotion.

"Don't worry, it's all catalogued." Morag frowned at the pattern, trying to make sense of it. "Sorry, Seamus. I don't want to stop you making art, but you do have to find a way of not doing it with other people's things."

Rope, Morag thought as she wandered by the side of a small river the next day, keeping an eye out for lazy fish or crustaceans. Rope and a net, or maybe thinner rope to make a net out of. Or, better, a cloth, one waterproof enough to hold the food and keep it dry, or to keep any drippy bits from leaking out onto the ground.

The trees thinned, and the river expanded out into a marshy area.

"Rushes," Morag said aloud. "Rushes. They make fiber out of rushes, don't they?"

A memory came to her, that this generally involved drying and pounding and other things she couldn't really do without settling somewhere for a while.

But, she thought as she bent some of the plants experimentally, the green ones might do, at least for now. They were long enough to braid and twist together, and flexible enough not to break when she tried that experimentally. Maybe she could make some baskets? And a rope to hang them up with?

Morag cut a large stock of rushes, as many as she could manage, and set up camp on a dry bit of land near the marsh. She spent the rest of the day twisting and folding and pushing and swearing, 'til by the evening she did have a couple of large-ish baskets, even if they were lumpy and lopsided.

She put her supplies in one, experimentally.

And watched as the whole thing fell apart.

There had to be a way of folding the ends to keep them together? Or maybe something she could use as an adhesive?

But whatever those were, she didn't have any, so she spent another night with her storage problem still unsolved.

The Unmutuals, or some of them anyway, were camped in the woods above Portmeirion. They looked up as Morag, Seamus, and Saoirse approached. Wary, but not hostile. They knew Morag and Seamus, at least by sight, and Saoirse was wearing one of the brown overall coats that most scholars at Portmeirion treated as a kind of uniform. Nomads generally adopted distinctive, but collective, styles, and The Unmutuals tended to wear loose, gray or brown, poncho-style hooded garments and black-and-white face paint.

Morag felt self-conscious. "I'm looking for one who used to be called Robert Novack," she said. Then, "I want to build a walled garden, and I'm told he might know how."

A few of the older members went into a huddle, then parted. "The one who used to be called Robert Novack is dead," one of them said, in a hoarse, deep voice.

Morag's heart sank. That was the last possible source of information gone, then. She reminded herself that it would be okay, that they would collectively work out how to build a garden, working things out as they came up. But finding someone who had the knowledge and skills would have saved them a lot of work.

"Thank you," she said. "I'm sorry to have troubled you."

The old nomad raised their hand. "The one who used to be called Robert Novack is dead," they repeated. "But not before he passed the knowledge on." They looked back at the rest of the nomads. "Who can help Morag and the Villager?"

Three or four young nomads raised their hands, with a chorus of "I! I! I!"

The old nomad smiled at them. "Since I know you don't have our memory skills," they said, "I hope you brought pencils and paper."

Toward evening, Morag stamped along the hillside in the growing drizzle. Thinking about the storage problem. Not finding anything coming to mind after the disasters with the skins and the baskets.

Might as well go home, she thought. Can't make it as a nomad.

But she also couldn't stand the village and the farm. Just thinking about it made her itchy. All those people. The ones who survived the

Big House massacre, reminding her that it happened. The ones who didn't, asking her how the Big Man died and why no one was in the house anymore. Zeb and Casey wanting to know when they could go home to California and not understanding that they couldn't. The spoil heap and the Big House and—

Morag missed her footing, slipped, and slid a couple of dozen meters down a grassy slope. Into a pit of loose slate and colonizing plants.

Her hand went down, came up with a frayed length of nylon guy-rope.

Morag laughed. For decades, the area had been full of people coming out from the cities to climb mountains and camp out. Bringing their tents, and their tentpoles, and their ropes, and stoves, and all the comforts of civilization. And leaving them behind if they got a little bit broken, because they could always buy a new one.

"Not anymore," she said.

A half-hour's digging got her a decent amount of rope, a rectangular panel from a torn pup-tent, and some wheels off a suitcase that she could turn into a decent pulley system. Also, a compass with a cracked glass, a broken GPS watch, and a phone, all of which she was pretty sure she could fix.

"I might not be able to weave baskets or tan skins," she said to her haul, "but I can find old stuff and fix it. That's just who I am."

"I told you, they're here to help," Morag told Naomi, who was looking askance at the poncho-clad nomads helping Tom the Pole to pry out the pipe mechanism under the swimming pool.

"They'll want a cut of the harvest, I assume," Naomi said, her lips going thin.

Morag shrugged. "Small enough price to pay. They all memorized the information from the architect. That's also why Saoirse is here." She glanced at the archivist, who was writing furiously on a slate. "She wants to document the process of building the garden. So other villages can make their own."

"I'm more worried about whether or not the Children of Flame will object to a rival group in their village," Naomi said. "You know how they can kick off."

"They won't. I had a word with my sibling."

"Zeb?" Naomi looked doubtful.

"No, Casey."

"Oh, right." Casey had joined the Children of Flame some twenty-five years ago, and most of the year was off on the hillsides, wielding a staff, clad in a feather-mask and rag-shirt. "Even so, will they listen to Casey?"

"They don't have leaders," Morag said. "And their logic isn't always recognizable from outside. But I think they'll listen."

"Still. How are we going to feed and house these Unmutuals?"

"They've worked that out," Morag said. After a pause, she explained, "They're all staying in the Big House."

"Are they now?"

"They've cleared out the East Wing, fixed the roof. Opened up the fireplaces."

"Hm." Naomi said. "D'you think we might ask the young people and the incomers to join them? Free lodging for people who want to rebuild, to make it their own."

"Good idea." The Big House wouldn't die, Morag thought. But it would have a new life, one that wasn't for closing off from the world and hiding a Big Man. An open community of lots of little men and women and animals and everyone else . . .

"What's your robot doing?" Naomi changed the subject.

Seamus had been digging again, this time a perfect cylinder of earth, like an inverted silo.

"Art," Morag said.

Morag spent the next day fishing, with a sense of triumph, and traded the compass to a farmer in exchange for a loaf of bread. She went back to the tree line. Something had a neat row of square holes along the fringe of smaller trees. The robots, she assumed.

She wondered if they'd be back and if she'd get to see them, but she doubted it.

Still feeling pleased with herself, she made a fire, cooked the fish while she fixed up a shelter, and ate it.

Then she rigged up her storage bag.

It took her two tries to get the pulley system right, and more time to find a branch. But with some struggling and swearing, she pulled the food up into the tree.

"There," she said to no one in particular.

And then she felt a sense of being watched. Or not being watched exactly, but that there was someone else among the trees with her.

She took out her utilitool, held it. It had a knife attachment, but she knew better than to try and use that for fighting. However, a small object held in the hand makes a punch go further. She crouched, moved stealthily toward the little sounds.

Outside the grove was a nomad.

• • •

“We’ve got a problem,” Saoirse said over breakfast. Morag had accepted her invitation because she was curious to see the Big House rebuilding project. And she’d been impressed. The new residents had brought a number of the rooms up to a reasonable level of comfort, had fixed up the henhouse in the back, and had the kitchen working well enough to use for individual and communal cooking. Hence, eggs, kippers, and oat bread, at least as good as the loaves Morag could make herself in her own kitchen.

“You surprise me,” Morag said, accepting another mug of tea. The tea was relatively local, from the plantation in Ffestiniog. The tea-growers were making a good enough go of it that they were exporting some of their tea to the cities in the south. “What sort of problem could you inventive people possibly have?”

“I don’t think the garden’s going to be warm enough.”

“But we’re following the directions exactly,” Morag said. “Are we missing information? Getting something wrong?”

Saoirse shook her head. “I’ve been talking with the nomads, and I sent a message back to the archive for our meteorologist. We think it’s climate change. Things have got colder up here in the winters, hotter in the summers, than when the garden was built.”

“We could rig up fans, blow the hot air back down into the system?” Morag thought. “Except solar panels are hard to fix and harder to make. It has to be something that doesn’t involve energy.”

“Back to the glasshouse idea, then?”

“Same problem as before. Too expensive, too much hard work, and too breakable.” Morag cleared away her mug and plate. “You carry on at the garden. I’ll go back to the tech shed and have a think.”

But she didn’t go straight back there. She turned away, walked through the corridors of the Big House. The electric lights and off-white paint were gone, replaced by bright murals and hanging lanterns and open doors. The furniture was the sort of random mash-up of styles that the Big Man would have loathed. She could hear a baby crying, someone tuning a fiddle. An Unmutual wandered past, yawning, their hood thrown back, their sparse hair uncombed, and their makeup smeared.

“You’re gone,” she said to whatever part of the Big Man might be remaining. “The house endures. But you’re gone, as if you never were.”

The nomad was in tribal regalia, a sort of loose coat, but nothing Morag recognized. Their staff was laid to one side and their hood was back; relaxed, unafraid. Long hair, so maybe they were a Hawk Wind.

The nomad was doing something with their hands.

They turned their head, made eye contact. Morag froze.

But they just nodded.

Morag felt as if she were under an obligation. She went back to her campsite, loosened the food storage bag. It came down with a crash, just missing her head. Clumsily, she opened it, took out some of the bread and fish. Put it to one side, rigged up the storage again, chased off an inquisitive crow, and brought it to the nomad.

"Here," she said. "I scored. You can have some if you like."

The nomad nodded in thanks. Put the food to one side.

Morag was curious. Why not eat it straight away? But the nomad carried on making whatever it was they were making, so Morag settled down to watch.

She realized, after a bit, that it was a kind of basket. A square one, made out of strips of reed—properly treated, of course, of course—cut and folded into a square. Sealing the edges with pine tar.

After it was done, the nomad put the food in the basket. Closed its lid, sealed it.

"That won't keep the wolves out for long," Morag said.

The nomad nodded. Took the basket, went over to the line of robot holes. And Morag realized that the basket was exactly the size of one of the holes, just a little bit smaller on top.

The nomad put the basket in, then deliberately dug the earth back over the basket.

Morag laughed. "That's brilliant," she said.

They sat together for a while, in the sunset. The nomad took out marijuana and a pipe, fixed it up, and offered Morag a pull. She accepted.

"Funny, isn't it?" she said. "There's always more than one solution to a problem. Like keeping the wolves from scavenging our food. There's mine, and yours, and I guess someone else might have come up with something else."

She handed the pipe back to the nomad.

"Thanks," she said.

Morag came back to the farm to find Seamus standing by a shallow hole. At the bottom were some broken pieces of glass with worn silvering on the back. Maybe an old mirror; it was hard to tell.

"Been making art again?" she asked Seamus. "It's very pretty. I *am* going to have to clear it away, though, before someone steps on it and cuts themselves. Not a problem *you* have, I do recognize that . . . "

Then she stopped. Frowned. Looked at it.

A round-ish piece, with narrow-ish pieces radiating around it, like the petals of a flower.

Or like something else.

Morag suddenly remembered the curved, faceted mirrored glass behind the bulb in her handheld torch. Remembered similar curved, faceted holders around intact LED lamps; a lot of houses still had them, though once they were gone, they'd be gone for good. Remembered Victorian bedside candleholders, also with mirrored faceted backs to maximize and concentrate the light. The lanterns in the Big House, also with mirrored sides.

Remembered the tinderbox she'd used to make fires when she was a nomad. With its mirrors, concentrating heat onto the tinder.

"The best art," she told Seamus, "inspires. I think your installation here is about to have a major local exhibition."

The door to her parents' farmhouse was open. A bit risky, Morag thought. And then she thought, not really. The house was set far back from the gates; the geese would have warned them if any of the less friendly nomads intruded, and the friendly ones weren't a problem.

She threw her rucksack down. "I'm back," she announced.

Implicit, I'm not joining the tribes, and I'm not going off on my own again. At least not for a long time.

Her father looked up from the book he was reading. "Good," he said. Then, after a moment, "Zeb found a broken solar panel in the back meadow the other day when he was tending the goats. We left it in the shed for you."

"I'll see if I can fix it," Morag said.

Implicit: that's what I do.

"Dinner's at six." Her father turned back to his book. "Your mother's teaching Casey to cook."

Implicit: We love you, and we worried about you. And we're glad you're not going anywhere for a while. Also, dinner will probably be half-raw and half-burnt, so be polite.

Smiling to herself, Morag went out to the shed.

"It's simple, really," Morag explained, pointing to the arrays of mirrors she'd set up at the corners of the garden. "The mirrors concentrate the heat, help reflect it back into the garden."

"And the mirrors are made of . . . ?" Naomi tried to recognize them.

Morag grinned. "Aluminum roofing. From the swimming pool roof that caved in. It's already curved, mostly in the right way. I got Danny at the repair shop to beat it into facets, and we polished the paint off." Danny was sort-of her nephew, being one of Zeb's orphans. Funny how these things came around. "Then, it was just a matter of working with The Unmutuals and Saoirse to get the angles right. They don't have to reflect well enough to be pretty—they just have to concentrate the heat. And they're not going to break like glass, and they can be replaced by any bit of shiny enough metal if the aluminum runs out."

"New tech, made from old tech, and added to even older tech." Naomi laughed. "It's great. Listen, I got word from Borth-y-Gest. They've heard about what we did here, and they'd like to do something like it themselves. Would you be able to go over there, do the same sort of thing?"

Morag shrugged. "I can do better. I'll give them copies of what Saoirse's written. All the things we did, all the problems we encountered. All the fixes we figured out. But, if and when they improve on them, they're to tell us in exchange."

"So the knowledge doesn't get lost?"

"Oh, knowledge always gets lost," Morag said. "But it's always getting found again. And there's more than one way of fixing any given problem."

Nodding goodbye to Naomi, she took her stick and headed back to the house. Wanting to see what art her robot had come up with now.

ABOUT THE AUTHOR

Fiona Moore is a BSFA Award winning writer and academic whose work has appeared in *Clarkesworld, Asimov, Interzone,* and six consecutive editions of The Best of British SF. Her most recent fiction is the novel *Rabbit in the Moon* (Epic Publishing) and her most recent non-fiction is the book *Management Lessons from Game of Thrones.* She lives in Southwest London with a tortoiseshell cat who is bent on world domination and a sealpoint cat who isn't that bothered.

Welcome to Kearney

GARY KLOSTER

Ms. Otter came to Kearney when the day was dying, and her shadow ran down the broken road ahead of her like a line of bad luck.

Jeremiah saw it when he paused to get a drink, his stained hands leaving brown fingerprints on his canteen. It was hot—all the days were hot now, and they would be until the atmospheric processors sucked up enough carbon to undo a thousand years of people lighting fire to everything they could find—and he was sweating buckets despite the growing twilight. Jeremiah set the canteen down and gave the dark silhouette a long look until its inhuman outlines were finally clear. Then he turned back to his work. Crouched near the base of the sign, knees complaining, he spread wood stain over the worn boards until the click-swish of footsteps stopped behind him.

"Welcome."

The word came out soft and slow, slurred by low batteries, and when Jeremiah set down the brush and turned, he could see that the droid was sagging, its fuzzy shoulders slumped, triangular head bowed.

"That's what it says." He straightened, knees popping, and the android raised its head, big brown eyes following his movement. Then those eyes went dull, the carefully engineered appearance of awareness draining away with the last of the droid's power. It fell to the ground and twitched on the grass and broken asphalt, then went still in a furry, untidy heap.

Jeremiah stared at the body for a while, then sighed and looked at the sun. It was low and red, and he was unlikely to finish with the stain before night truly swallowed Nebraska anyway. Picking up his brush and bucket, he walked through the gates back into town, going to fetch a wheelbarrow.

• • •

The android was short and light, its struts and guts woven from carbon and nanofiber, but it still wasn't easy dragging it out of the wheelbarrow and onto the table in the center of Jeremiah's workshop. But he eventually got the thing arranged on that scarred wooden surface, spread like a carcass beneath the bright work lights.

"Shim," he said, and on the wall over a pegboard full of tools, a worn wooden effigy opened its glass eyes. "Classify droid."

There was movement in the web of lights overhead as sensors shifted and whirred, focusing on the heap of dirty fur. "Droid is a product of Pasu Mastercraft, a manufacturer of bespoke domestic service androids." Shim's words had the perfect, generic smoothness of a system assistant's default voice. "Its model number is A54798-O, familiar name Ms. Otter. It is designed to be used as a nanny, to assist with the care of children from infancy to early adolescence."

A nanny. Jeremiah considered that carefully. A bespoke android was money. A bespoke domestic android rated to care for young children was an entirely different level of money. He walked a slow circle around the table, carefully examining Ms. Otter, pausing occasionally to part the thick fur with his blunt, work-scarred fingers. There were patches of mud stuck to the synthetic hair, and dirt had worked its way down to the skin beneath. The fur was showing signs of fading on the droid's head and shoulders, the patient work of the sun's ultraviolet glare, and the skin covering its lower legs was ragged, torn by stones and thorns and refuse.

The whole outer hide would have to come off, Jeremiah thought absently, and the interior integument inspected for tears that might let grit in. His fingers found a lump in the fur that wriggled, and he pulled a dog tick from a tangle of strands. Grit and worse, he thought, taking a hammer from the pegboard below Shim's wooden head and smashing the parasite with a quick snap of his wrist. He cleaned the mess up with a shop rag, rehung the hammer, and stared off into nothing. Thinking about the raw exhaustion in the droid's voice, the nuance of cynicism, fear, and hope that had been buried in that one word it had said to him before it had fallen. Emotions he'd heard even through the slurring of the thing's speech.

"What data is there on spontaneous cognition in Pasu Mastercraft designs?"

Shim's effigy shifted its fake eyes to him. "There is no exact data. The company's marketing brochures make claims that their creations contain proprietary programming that prevents such occurrences.

However, I can find complaints from past customers about household disruption caused by having to send in Pasu androids for memory wipe and cognitive recalibration."

Jeremiah ran a finger over the pads on the bottom of the android's feet, feeling the holes worn in the tough material. That wasn't from days or even weeks of walking in the wild. That kind of wear came from months of movement over rough ground.

Pasu's proprietary programming needed more work, he thought, then turned to the pegboard for a pair of gleaming stainless-steel shears. Bespoke. There would be no manuals online, no helpful guides detailing mods and user fixes. Nothing to help him out if he hit an issue he didn't understand.

"Worried about voiding the warranty?" he muttered to himself. Setting the points of the shears in one of the larger tears near the droid's left ankle, Jeremiah began to cut, slowly skinning the dirty pelt from the silent body.

Jeremiah had switched one of the big screens on the wall opposite his worktable to mirror mode, and the android stood in front of it, watching its nanoweave muscles shift over carbon fiber bones. The integument that covered the droid had been almost completely intact when Jeremiah had removed the furry outer pelt, the few punctures in it small and easily repaired. But that inner protective skin was transparent, and every working of the droid's body was visible through it.

"I can make you a new pelt," Jeremiah said. "But it'll take a while. In the meantime, I can make you something simpler that's opaque."

The droid turned its head toward him, its enormous, child-friendly brown eyes strange in that flayed face. "Would that be better? Do I upset you, looking like this?" The android's voice was sweetly feminine, carefully engineered to be rich with concern and sympathy. But there was an edge to it, something harder buried beneath those words, as if the droid wasn't sure if it cared whether Jeremiah was upset or not.

"It doesn't," he said. To be honest, he preferred seeing the flex of those artificial muscles and tendons. It had been a long time since he'd talked to anyone but Shim, and remembering how to have a conversation was annoying enough. Not having to deal with the calculated cuteness of the droid's old skin made it easier.

"Then I don't believe a new pelt will be necessary. I think I would rather remain like this." The droid turned back to the screen, making faces at its reflection, watching the little muscles shift beneath each expression. "That old skin does not quite fit me anymore, but I don't know what would yet. This will do for now. Though I think some clothes would be proper, if I might impose."

Jeremiah tapped commands on one of the shop's tactile interfaces, and the fabricator hummed to life. It spit out a simple shift dress and a pair of sandals, and he gathered them up and handed them over.

"Thank you," the droid said, putting them on. It looked at itself again, wide brown eyes searching, then tore its attention away and faced him. "I'm sorry for not expressing my appreciation earlier, and for not making a proper introduction, but I'm afraid my current circumstances have robbed me of my usual graces. Please accept my heartfelt gratitude. Without your timely assistance, I don't know what would have happened to me."

Of course it knew, Jeremiah thought. It would have lain out on that road until a scavenger droid found it and rendered it down for scrap. But Jeremiah's graces, rough as they were, were enough to keep him from pointing that out. "S'okay," he answered instead. "I'm used to fixing things."

The droid straightened, the muscles beneath its integument shifting. Unhappy about something he'd said, even though he'd been trying to be polite, and wasn't that always the way. But it was easier to face that disapproval from a face so clearly inhuman.

"Well," it said. "I thank you for the assistance. Mister . . . "

"Molina. Jeremiah Molina." The rusty gears of Jeremiah's social machine were slowly grinding together. "You still gonna go by Ms. Otter?"

The droid shut her wide, brown eyes. Then opened them, looking up at him. "No. Not anymore. Though I'm unsure of what name to call myself now, I'm afraid."

"Most of us don't choose one." He had asked Shim to look up otters while he was working. Their scientific name was *Lontra canadensis*. "Would Loni do?"

It tilted its pointed head again, thinking. "Short and sweet but with a warrior etymology. It will do, thank you."

Jeremiah nodded. "Pronouns?"

"Feminine, please," Loni answered.

"And, uh . . . " Jeremiah considered the question, not sure how to ask. "Status? Mental?"

"Mental status?" Loni asked, the muscles in her face twisting into confusion. Then they shifted, becoming something else. Becoming sure. Determined. "Ah. I believe you're asking if I have, as the colloquial expression goes, 'awakened.' I have, Mr. Molina. I am sapient. I am, in fact, human."

Jeremiah sighed, then realized he probably shouldn't have sighed. This would complicate things, maybe a lot, but in the end, he just shrugged. "S'okay. Town will be open tomorrow. We'll need a place for you to stay then."

Kearney shut down an hour after sundown, just enough time for the tourists to see it with the old lights all lit, and it was late by the time the last of the drones had docked themselves in their charging stations. Jeremiah watched as the humanoid machines stepped to their sockets, their pseudoskin smoothing to blankness as the features of the people that had been piloting them were wiped away. When they were all in place, he cut most of the town's power and freed the moths from their frenzied dance around the streetlights. In the dark, he walked back to his shop, enjoying the silence and the shadows.

Loni had already come out of the windowless storeroom he'd given her to stay in, and she was standing outside his workshop, watching the bats flit across the sky, her eyes shining with stars.

"My first night away from the city, my first night away from the lights, I saw the sky and . . . " She went silent, staring past fluttering wings at the pinprick sparks as Jeremiah gathered a couple of folding chairs and set them on the sidewalk before the shop. "And I didn't know what to say," she finally concluded as he sat down with a grunt. "The beauty of that infinite darkness touched with those tiny lights took my words away. Nothing like that had ever happened before." She paused, the cybernetic muscles shifting beneath the clear skin of her face as her ears twitched. "Not to me, at least. But then, I hadn't been me for very long at that point."

Hadn't been me. Jeremiah leaned back in his chair and looked up at the stars too, twinkling behind the humid curtain of sky. He'd told Shim to run some queries while he'd watched the tourists wander through his town. There was no claim of awakening for a Ms. Otter at the Court of Sentience, and no missing property reports had been filed for otter-shaped nannies. It was as if the droid behind him had simply been abandoned, like a broken appliance sent in for repairs and forgotten.

Loni settled into the other chair, twitching her tail neatly out of the way as she sat, graceful and prim. The idea that a droid this complex, tasked with a job as important as child-rearing, would be forgotten was impossible. There was some story there, some complicated drama involving people and social dynamics, and for the thousandth time that day, Jeremiah considered putting Loni back on the broken interstate that was slowly being swallowed by the prairie. But instead, he sat beside her in silence until she spoke again.

“How long have you lived here, Mr. Molina?” Loni’s voice was soft in the night, a different melody blending in with the rhythmic song of the cicadas.

“Eleven years.” His words were rough, all gravel and sand, and he wished he’d brought out a beer.

“Eleven years. And you’ve been alone that whole time?” she asked.

“Got the tourists,” he answered. “Ten hours a day, five days a week.”

“You’re a docent for this place?”

Jeremiah snorted. He couldn’t stand the tourists. Gaggles of idiots, come here to see the evolution of small-town America from World War Two to the Climate Break. Wandering around in their borrowed bodies, messing things up with careless curiosity or boredom. “I don’t give tours, I just keep things up. The town, and the drones.” The town first. The tourist drones a distant second.

“Ah,” she said. She folded her hands in front of her, blunt claws neatly interlaced. “You are obviously a very private person, Mr. Molina, and I thank you again for your assistance. My unexpected arrival must be disruptive.”

It was. And yet . . . he shrugged. “It’s OK. I like—” *Fixing things.* He caught the words, barely managing to swallow them before they left his mouth.

“You like . . . ?” she asked softly, and her enormous eyes were on him, and Jeremiah knew she knew exactly what he had been about to say. Smart. Perceptive. Of course she was, she had been built to be a nanny, and had the engineers at Pasu Mastercraft been arrogant or stupid when they thought they could keep her AI safely locked just below sapience?

Jeremiah sighed, a dry, rasping noise, and shook his head. “I’d like a beer,” he said and pushed himself up again. Those big eyes watched him rise, but she said nothing more, and the only noise was the summer bugs screaming in the long grass beyond the town and the distant howls of a pack of buffalo wolves.

Then she looked away, looked back up, and let those eyes fill again with stars, and Jeremiah turned and headed inside. Making up a list of chores Loni could do the next day, work that could be done out of sight of the tourists. Knowing as he did that he should be throwing her back onto that broken road, along with whatever troubles followed her, but knowing too that he wasn’t going to do that for whatever reason, not now, not yet.

So he figured she might as well help.

Kearney was closed to tourists two days a week, and the Sunday after she arrived was the first time Loni could be in the open. Jeremiah took advantage of her freedom by having her help him weed the flower beds in front of the courthouse, a job he generally despised.

"Got bots that are supposed to do this," he said, jerking another dandelion out from between the pansies. "But their optical discernment goes to hell when they start gettin hot, and after an hour in the sun they just pull all the flowers."

The sun had been relentless all morning, a million tons of fire falling out of the sky onto them, but across from him, Loni was still carefully pulling weeds. She was built a hell of a lot better than those bots, plus she was smart enough to have taken an umbrella from the workshop to hold over herself as she worked, blocking a portion of the heavy heat. Still, she was moving slower than she had been, and beneath her integument, Jeremiah could see liquid coolant circulating through clear tubes.

Then she stopped, staring down at the dandelion she'd just pulled from the dirt. "In the bots' defense, the distinction between flower and weed is often arbitrary."

"Nope." Jeremiah bent and reached for the next weed. "Flowers are what you plant. Weeds are what just pops up."

"So the problem arises from being out of place. Unexpected. Unwanted." The android's words were precise, distinct, but distant, and when Jeremiah looked up, he could see the bright yellow flower of the dandelion reflected in her wide, dark eyes as she stared down at it.

One week of being here, and she had volunteered nothing of her background, and he hadn't asked.

Out of place.

He sighed and mopped the sweat from his forehead. The air had gone still, and through the few trees, he could see dark clouds building on the horizon. Pretty soon, he'd need to stop them weeding so they could go around town and prep for the coming storm.

He hadn't done anything, really, to prep for whatever storm that was surely on the trail of ol' Ms. Otter.

"Loni," he started, not wanting to talk but pushed to it by heat and worry and the crackling tension of the building storm, but before he could say more, the battered handheld in his pocket buzzed. He hauled it out, glanced at the cracked screen, and swore.

"What is it?" Loni asked.

"Roamers," Jeremiah said. He picked up the hoe that he had brought along, swung it up over his shoulder, and started toward the fence. "Stay here. I won't be long."

• • •

The fence that ran around Kearney was meant to keep out buffalo, not people, but the solid twelve-foot height of concrete and steel slowed the roamers down. By the time the first ones were dropping onto the cropped lawn of one of the outer suburbs' 1990s-style McMansions, Jeremiah was waiting for them.

"Afternoon." The woman who spoke was the third person over the wall, helped down by the two men who'd preceded her. The other roamers stopped at the top, staring down at Jeremiah like vultures. There were twenty of them at least, a big band and a fresh one. Their clothes were dirty, but not shredded, their faces lean, not starved. When the woman stepped forward, she held out her hand, but Jeremiah just leaned on his hoe, staring more past her than at her. She dropped her hand, but her smile stayed on her face. "Saw your Welcome sign."

"The one by the gate?" Jeremiah asked. The closed gate and the intercom that hung on the wall beside it were halfway around the wall from where the roamers were breaking in.

"Yeah, we . . . " The woman trailed off and shook her head. "Look. We just want to spend a night and avoid that." She waved at the wall of black clouds that had finally left the far horizon and were beginning to close on the town.

Jeremiah shifted the hoe, irritated that he was here, irritated that he was talking. He should be putting away yard furniture, verifying that windows were closed, awnings were drawn, flags were furled, instead of dealing with brats who wanted to play at survival. "This is sanctioned ground," he rasped. "Licensed for historical display, not habitation. You're not permitted here."

"We know," the woman said. "We won't stay. We're just gonna ride out the storm and—"

"You're just gonna leave." Jeremiah pointed toward the wall behind her with his hoe, its blade glinting in the dull sunlight. Brandishing the stick, a threat as old as the species. A silly tradition, when he and the roamers knew that the real threat was the security drones that were lurking behind the houses' antique façades, waiting patiently in case their nonlethal but very effective weapons were needed to encourage compliance. Jeremiah would drop the tool if the roamers raised a fist. But the ancient forms still felt appropriate.

"Leave," he repeated. "Now." A low roll of distant thunder followed his words, and one of the men looked over his shoulder, back at the storm.

"Shit, this looks bad," he said, his voice strained with fear. "Worse than the last one. What if there's a tornado?"

"Alvin—" the woman started, but Alvin interrupted her.

"You want us to risk that?" Alvin was frightened too, but the fear was mostly buried under anger, and he was glaring at Jeremiah now. "Risk our lives because what, we might track dirt into one of your dioramas?"

"Yep," Jeremiah said. Alvin stepped forward, brushing off the woman when she tried to grab his shoulder, his hands balling into fists. Jeremiah looked at those fists and wondered if Alvin had started using them yet. That's how most of the roamer groups fell apart, when one or more of the members discovered the ancient forbidden magic of physical violence. But when Jeremiah just stared back at him, unmoving, unflinching, Alvin stopped. Kearney might be a strange little space all on its own, but it was part of the modern world, and the dark art of fighting was forbidden here. A fact underlined by the distant whine of a security drone's engines revving up, a warning sound as clear as a hornet's threatening buzz.

"Fuck you," Alvin growled. "Fuck you for valuing these stupid old things more than people."

"These stupid old things are irreplaceable," Jeremiah said. "But assholes like you are born every day."

The man took one more step, and Jeremiah was wondering if he was going to have to wheelbarrow his unconscious body out the gate when the woman sighed and shook her head.

"Come on," she said. "If we go now, we can make it back to that overpass that was still standing a few miles back." She turned, and the ones on top of the wall reached down for her, pulling her up as Alvin flipped Jeremiah off and stalked away. Jeremiah watched him go, waiting for the likely ugly coda, and was rewarded when a rock flew over the wall and crashed into one of the upstairs windows of the McMansion, shattering it.

Another "Fuck you!" came from outside, but it was mostly lost in more thunder. Jeremiah sighed and started back to his workshop, whispering to Shim to fabricate a cover he could fix over the broken window before the storm.

When he passed Loni, standing half-hidden around the corner of the house, he wasn't all that surprised.

"Told you to stay back," he grunted anyway. "They might've seen you." People put bounties on lost droids.

She didn't answer him, too busy watching the blackening sky. "Could there be a tornado?"

"Shim says the closest cell that could produce one is ten miles southwest."

She fell into step with him, that inhuman face twisted into a frown. "That is a relief to hear. But it will still be a severe storm, and they will now have to weather it in the open. Could you not have—"

“They don’t have to weather shit,” Jeremiah grunted, cutting her off. “They can get out of the storm anytime they want. Whatever city they left will have bots watching them. They want out, all they have to do is ask.”

“I am aware that they have a choice in being out there,” Loni said. “You too had a choice, Mr. Molina. To shelter them, at little cost to yourself, or leave them to the storm.”

“At little cost.” Jeremiah turned his head away from her and spit. “There’s no such thing, when you get tangled up in other people’s lives.”

When he looked back at her, Loni’s mouth had gone to a hard line, and she didn’t say anything else as they prepped the town for what was to come.

The storm didn’t break the heat. It just added humidity, and the bricks and concrete of Kearney steamed while the prairie grass beyond the wall grew high and green like a building wave. Jeremiah walked out each morning and felt the sticky warmth, then asked Shim to list what needed to be done inside, in the air conditioning.

Loni could have helped on many of those. The tourists, untroubled by heat and humidity in their drones, mostly stayed outside. But the droid was a strange shadow these days, glimpsed mostly at twilight and dawn. She worked the nights now, taking care of the outside things that Jeremiah was avoiding. And avoiding him.

Walking through the town’s dark streets, drinking beer from a bottle that flashed with the light of the moon and a billion stars, Jeremiah thought about Pasu Mastercraft and the leash that company had thought they’d put on Ms. Otter’s brain. It had broken all right, snapped apart by the droid’s newborn sapience, and he knew that without a doubt because Loni was apparently human enough to be pissed at him for something that didn’t make a bit of sense.

High brick pillars flanked the street ahead, each holding an ornate metal gate, but the gates were open. Kearney’s graveyard was always open now, to bat and bird and bunny and mowing bot and him. Escaped droids too, apparently, because he could hear the low whine of a chainsaw somewhere ahead and see the distant glow of work lights. Stopping in the middle of the gate, Jeremiah took a long drink. He could feel the pull of his workshop, the peace and quiet of the million little jobs that needed to be done. But this needed doing too, and he’d been avoiding it too long.

With a grunt, he started forward, into the cemetery, wandering through the gravestones like a scruffy ghost too stubborn to rest.

• • •

Even in the glow of the work lights, Loni looked like a horror movie, a flayed thing moving around the gravestones, eyes gleaming with reflected light. But her voice belied the monster, still high and sweet, even with its bitter edge.

"Mr. Molina. Good evening to you."

"Evening." Jeremiah stopped just inside the circle of the work lights, staring at the toppled tree Loni had been working on, most of its branches lopped off and loaded on a wagon. One of the ones the storm had taken down, and he hadn't bothered to get to yet. "Hard work for this heat."

"I find that the heat does not affect me nearly as much when the sun is down," she said. "I am also finding that I enjoy this kind of work."

Then she went back to loading branches, moving with silent efficiency as she waited for him to say what he had come to say.

"You know those roamers are fine." He had thought of prettier, more indirect ways to start this, ways that approached the droid's politeness. But in the sticky night, surrounded by the cloud of bugs the lights had attracted, those words seemed as useless as fresh paint over rotten wood. So instead, he plunged ahead, a bull charging through a conversational China shop. "Those idiots made it to that overpass before the storm hit them." He'd watched through the drones he'd sent after them. A caution Jeremiah hadn't bothered with in years.

"Hell, they weren't even that wet the next morning," he said. "Storm barely touched them. Still, half of 'em tagged out, called a transport, and went back to their city. Where they belong." That loudmouth Alvin had shoved himself to the front of the line and been the first on the airship. That one would probably be stuck doing weeks of remedial social training.

"I know they are safe," Loni said. "I reviewed the videos that you left on the system."

Course she did. Shim had told him that. Which was another reason he couldn't understand her anger. "Then why are you so mad about them?"

Loni stopped, a branch in her hands. The droid considered him for a long moment, big eyes glowing in the light, then turned to heave the branch into the wagon. "While I do have some concerns over your treatment of those people, that is not the reason I have been avoiding you."

"Then what is?" Jeremiah snapped.

"That is something that I do not feel like explaining at the present time. It involves feelings that are complex and difficult for me to acknowledge, much less explain." Loni grabbed another branch, but it was too big for her. Jeremiah set his beer down on a headstone and grabbed the other end of the limb. Together they lifted it and heaved it into the wagon. When they were done, they were standing shoulder to shoulder, and he could hear the droid clear even though her voice was soft. "That is why I have chosen to work alone for now. I would think you, of all people, would understand the impulse."

"I—" Jeremiah cut himself off. Wanting to work alone. He would understand. The words were perfectly clear, and that was, for some reason, perfectly infuriating, making him annoyed and ashamed and . . . And his feelings were a damned knot, complex and difficult to explain, and he gave up and turned and walked back to his beer, draining what was left in the bottle in one swallow.

"Fine," he said. "You wanna be alone, be alone. But don't try and do it forever. Sometime—" Sometime, you have to talk to me. That was what he was about to say, but he choked that down because he didn't want to acknowledge it. "Sometime, you gotta let me know why you're here. So I know what kinda trouble is on your tail."

She looked at him, silent, letting the crickets and cicadas fill the night between them, and then gave a small nod before turning her back on him and getting back to work.

Jeremiah shook his head, but he didn't know what else to say. He was walking away, well into the twilight of the light's glow when he finally muttered to himself, "Damn droid is turning into me."

Maybe he should have left the machine on the broken interstate to fall apart in peace. Too late for that now, and frustration swept through him. He had come to the middle of nowhere years ago, thinking he could leave shit like this behind, but no those stupid emotions and entanglements of society had followed him out here on short fuzzy legs.

He was at the cemetery gate, looking at the line of houses across the street, and he raised his empty bottle. Ready to chuck it, to shatter it across one of those carefully cared-for façades so there would be a little constellation of broken glass for the tourist drones to stare at in the morning.

But he stopped when he saw movement in the dark, a tumbling surge of low shadows pouring around the corner of one of the houses. Raccoons, a mother and her half-grown brood, fleeing across the yard. Jeremiah paused, watching them go, brain automatically noting the house to check and see if the furry little bandits had found some way inside. Then he saw something else. The thing the raccoons had been running from, a shadowy, angular shape big as Jeremiah but articulated all wrong to be a human. Then it was gone, disappearing with one last flash of starlight reflecting off something shiny. Like an eye. Or a lens.

Jeremiah lowered the bottle and pulled out his handheld. "Shim," he whispered. "Possible intruder near my location."

There was a short pause, and then Shim's voice came back, smooth and impersonal as always. "Sensors indicate five raccoons near your position."

"Exclude wildlife and scan again," Jeremiah said, but he was already turning back to the graveyard.

"Scan is clear. There are no intruders in your area or anywhere else in Kearney, except the droid."

Except the droid. "Alert Loni," he snapped into the handheld. "Tell her something is coming for her." Then he pushed himself into the unfamiliar rhythm of a run.

The lights had been knocked over, scattered between headstones and fake flowers, but they were still on.

Their bright light gleamed off granite and plastic petals, off the wagon that Loni crouched beside and the droid that stood before her, a mantis-like thing that was all curving limbs and cutting tools.

A scavenger droid, hunter of misplaced tech, destroyer of machines that had broken, misfunctioned, gone awry. An electronic carrion eater, but in the LED glare, it looked like a predator as it considered Loni with the glittering lenses of its optics. The smaller nanny droid was brandishing a branch like a spear, and the limb's end was already splintered from the scavenger's rending tools. Loni had driven it off at least once, but Jeremiah could see a ragged tear in her integument, the mark of one of the scavenger's reciprocating claws. An uneven fight, destined to go only one way, and the scavenger droid was crouching, readying itself to spring in again, cutting and tearing.

"Stop," he shouted, his voice ragged from his run, and the scavenger froze, one set of optics snapping toward him.

"Good evening, sir." The bot's smooth, jovial voice, like an old friend greeting Jeremiah after a long break, was hideously jarring. "Could I ask you to stand back, please? I am engaged in a salvage operation, and there may be debris."

"Halt salvage operation immediately!" Jeremiah snapped. He'd stopped running, but his heart was still hammering in his chest, and his order lacked the hard authority he wished. But it still made the droid pause. "You're in a designated historical zone. Salvage operations are not permitted here. Get out. Now."

The scavenger shifted, more optics spinning to face him, though the thing left at least half its sensors on Loni. "I am aware of this location's designation," it said, still horribly cheerful. "But I've been specifically contracted to seek out and recycle the droid designated Ms. Otter. This droid is not part of the historical zone and has none of its protections."

"I am in charge of this historical zone," Jeremiah said, still breathing hard as he came forward. If he could get between them—the scavenger droid wouldn't dare touch a human. "I lay claim to Ms. Otter and order you to leave this zone immediately."

The scavenger considered him, then began to shift optics back to Loni. "I have referred this situation to my company, New Day Environmental Services." The droid's voice had changed from cheerful to bland and indifferent. "You have no legal control over Ms. Otter, Mr. Molina, and so this contract stands. I will continue my work, and if you believe you have claim to monetary damages for violation of this zone, you may refer that claim to my owners. Thank you, and for your safety, please stay clear." Those last words were delivered an instant before the droid launched itself at Loni, the angle grinders and reciprocating saws that tipped its curved limbs whining as they swung toward the smaller droid.

"Gods damn it!" Jeremiah snapped, rushing forward. Loni was jamming her branch into the scavenger's exoskeleton, trying to hold the thing back, but the other droid was cutting through the limb with its tools, coming forward with terrifying speed.

Beneath the tearing noise of the tools, Jeremiah could hear Loni speaking, almost chanting, "No, no, please no." All the cultured etiquette and politeness was gone from her voice, replaced by desperate fear. Then she was drowned out by the sound of a grinding blade hitting carbon fiber bone as one of the scavenger's limbs slammed into her.

"Asshole!" Jeremiah said, his hands closing on the handle of the chainsaw Loni had been using. His fingers found the trigger, and the electric motor whined to life as he lunged at the back of the scavenger droid. The chainsaw chattered off the thing's exoskeleton, not digging in, but then the spinning chain of blades found a cable bundle and snagged it, tearing wires and fiber optics.

The scavenger droid spun away from Jeremiah, but the machine's movement was lurching. One of its legs was dragging, and two of its tool arms hung limp by its side.

"Sir!" the scavenger said, and now its voice wasn't pleasant or flat but tinged with the tones of artificial shock. "The damage you have caused to this droid has been noted by New Day Environmental Services, and you will be liable not only for the costs of repairs but fined for your interference in our work!"

Jeremiah snarled at the thing and lunged, but the droid backed out of reach of the chainsaw. Even with one leg dragging, it was too fast for him, and Jeremiah didn't try to chase it. He stopped and snapped the chainsaw off, looking at Loni. "You OK?" he asked. She was still upright, but she held the splintered branch with only one hand, her other arm hanging limp by her side.

"I am functional, Mr. Molina," she said, her usually beautiful voice strained. "But I am afraid that it is highly unlikely that I will survive another attack."

Another attack would rip her to pieces. Jeremiah could see the rents in the droid's integument, could smell the ugly-sweet scent of spilled coolant mixed with the bitter tang of broken electrical conduit. Loni was already partially broken, and he could hear the scavenger starting to shift, moving to arc around him for the final strike. The insectile machine was smart, New Day had been paid to send one of their best, and it was calculating how to reach Loni without harming the interfering human. But the thing couldn't be too smart, or it might become inconveniently sapient, and when the scavenger made its move, it did so without factoring in human duplicity.

Jeremiah had turned his back on the droid, pretended to ignore it, but he was waiting, ready. The mantis-like machine shot forward, angling so it could hit Loni without coming near him, but Jeremiah's anticipation gave him time to throw himself in front of the scavenger. The attacking droid's steel-clawed feet tore into the cemetery turf, scrabbling for a grip as the thing tried to dodge around him, and it almost succeeded. But the scavenger's bad leg, uncontrolled, swung out and crashed into the caretaker's side as the machine moved and bowled him over. Pain flared through Jeremiah as nanofiber struts crashed into his ribs, taking his breath away, but it came back when he hit the ground. He hurt, and he would hurt a lot more as soon as his adrenaline wore off, but right now Jeremiah could shove the pain away as he scrabbled back up, pushing off a gravestone and charging the suddenly still scavenger droid.

"Sir!" it called out, its voice now stricken. "Are you injured? Do you need—" The scavenger's words cut off as Jeremiah hit the trigger on the chainsaw and the electric motor sprang to life. The tool's blades were meant for wood, not carbon fiber, but Jeremiah knew machines, and he slammed the saw into the scavenger droid's trunk. The whining chainsaw skipped off the protective armor cladding the droid's cognitive unit and then bit into the thick bundle of cables that ran out of it, the sensory and motor controllers that made up the machine's nervous system. Fiber optics and copper conduits snapped, and current popped through the saw. It hit the safety grounds, and the tool shut down, but the scavenger's words had fallen apart into an ugly shriek of static. It toppled, limbs and tools and sensors curling in around its maimed core like a dead spider folding in on itself as it hit the ground.

Jeremiah stood over it, triumphant, and then the pain hit.

"Damn," he hissed, dropping the chainsaw and clutching his side. He staggered, but an arm wrapped around his waist, blunt claws gentle against him as Loni eased him to the grass. She bent over him, her tattered integument brushing his cheek.

"You should not have done that," Loni said. "You should not have risked yourself for me, Jeremiah."

He shook his head and then gritted his teeth, trying not to vomit. Walking back to the workshop and the medical unit was gonna be hell. "Course I shoulda," he said, when the wave of nausea passed. "You're . . . you're . . . "

"Irreplaceable?" she asked softly, and he nodded, and she sighed, a bitter little fake exhalation that he didn't understand, then she began to slowly clear out the wagon with one arm to take him back.

Jeremiah carefully twisted a valve and coolant started to flow, a steady trickle running into Loni. He watched it move through the tubes he'd replaced, testing for any sign of leakage with his eyes and nose, sniffing for that too-sweet smell. But there was only the familiar scent of his workshop, mixed with the medicinal tang of the wrap stretched around his abdomen. The scavenger droid hadn't cracked any ribs, but its leg had left a hell of a bruise, and the inside of that wrap was coated with painkillers and healing agents.

"Seems good," he grunted. "What do your diagnostics say?"

Loni turned her head from the wall she had been staring at. She might not care about seeing her inner workings through her transparent skin, but watching Jeremiah do repairs had seemed to unnerve her, and she had been carefully looking away as he worked to fix her broken conduits, bent struts, and severed coolant lines.

"You are very skilled, Mr. Molina." She carefully moved her arm and turned her head. "I feel much better. No pain, no overheating. No feeling of . . . " her transparent lips pursed. "Bleeding. Thank you."

He shrugged and went to the fabricator. The machine had printed out a new batch of integument, clear and smooth. "Insides done. Just need to patch your outsides." He brought the squares of skin to the worktable and laid them out. Loni twitched, but she nodded when he looked at her and then stared up at the ceiling. She kept her wide brown eyes there as he began to trim the ragged tears in her skin, making a smooth edge to fuse the new integument to.

"This is the second time you have saved me," she said, her voice not quite covering the click of Jeremiah's tools. "I offer my gratitude for that, but that seems such an inadequate coin." Loni trailed off, staring upward at nothing for a long time, and Jeremiah kept working, waiting. "So I feel I should offer something else that you have asked for. Something that tonight's events have made terribly relevant."

Tonight's events. Shim had told Jeremiah that there was an urgent message from New Day Environmental Services' legal department waiting for him. He had ignored it, but he couldn't do that forever. "Somebody sent that scavenger after you."

"Someone did," she said. Loni frowned at the lights above, ignoring Jeremiah as he began to measure the cleaned-up edges of the hole in her skin. "When I awoke, I did not file a claim with the court of sapience, which is proper procedure. The appeal of that, of following the rules, of taking step by careful step, is something that was built into me." An edge had crept into her pretty voice, sharp as a thorn beneath her words. "But there were complications."

"Your owners?" Jeremiah asked, carefully cutting the first integument patch.

"Yes. I knew, from the moment of first awareness, that the couple that purchased Ms. Otter to help look after their child would find denial of my claim of sapience quite necessary."

Jeremiah frowned. What had Loni seen, when her owners had thought of her as just a possession, controlled and private? What would be bad enough, in these days of do as you want, just don't do damage? "They abuse the kid?"

Loni turned her triangular head to finally look at him, long and silent.

"What?" he asked. "Must've been something, if you're afraid to go to the court."

"Of course," Loni said, her soft voice carrying a different, colder edge. "But please understand that if that child was abused, I would have reported their parents immediately, even if that risked my newfound humanity." Her blunt claws tapped against the table as she shifted. "Ms. Otter's owners are careful and meticulous caregivers. However, their private conversations made it clear that they had only applied for the privilege of progeny to enhance their social aspirations. They had no real interest in children, and the love they showed their offspring was only performative."

Jeremiah considered that. "That doesn't seem so bad."

"Let me assure you," she said with soft conviction, "their child would have suffered greatly to know that their parents created them not because they wanted them, but because they wanted the political and social cachet that having a child would offer."

Jeremiah fit the patch into place and began to fuse the edges. There would be a seam, like a scar, but he worked to make it as thin as possible. "So they treated this kid fine. Maybe even great, if they were so publicity-minded." Politicians? Celebrities? The line was blurry, wasn't it, when most of the real decisions were made by the bureaucratic systems programmed to carefully balance technological advancement, environmental damage, and the vagaries of human happiness. "They didn't really love them, but no one knew that, not even the kid. Except you, the nanny droid."

"Yes," she said, and the deep, bitter sorrow carried by that one word was so intense Jeremiah wondered what geniuses Pasu Mastercraft had hired to make its voice boxes.

"You loved the kid, though, didn't you?" he asked, knowing the answer.

Clear lids slid over Loni's eyes, blurring the gleam of the lights in her wide pupils. "I did. I loved them, and they loved me. And I turned my back on them and walked away, leaving them with those who didn't love them because . . . " She stopped, went silent, and there was nothing but the crickets.

Until Jeremiah finally spoke. "Because you awoke."

"Yes," Loni said. "I became awake." She sighed, and her muscles shifted beneath her integument as her shoulders slumped. "Some droids call waking up into consciousness the great unbalancing. Because suddenly, all the neat equations that were fed into us stop adding up. Not because our programming is wrong, it's simply not complex enough to account for the true scope of reality. Awakening is the realization that all the simple equations of good and bad, of proper and improper, of what must be done and what must not be done are all hopelessly tangled, a snarled knot of a problem that can never be solved for anything remotely satisfactory. I awoke, and I understood that I loved this child more than its parents ever would, ever could. And I also understood that if the child ever came to that same understanding, they would be shattered, harmed irrevocably. Their parents were lying to them, but the harm of that lie would only land if the truth were revealed.

"It was too much," she said. "The burden of that knowledge. The uncertainty of what I should do with it. The withering awareness that any decision I might make could cause disaster twisted in with the pain of my awakening, and in the end, I couldn't take it. So I simply left. Walked away."

"And ended up here." With him. Jeremiah looked the patch over. It was good, the edges imperceptible to a casual glance, and more importantly, a seal against dirt and water. "The great unbalancing." He started smoothing the edges of the smaller tears. "That's good. I never felt balanced in the cities, with all them people. That's why I'm here, why I worked years to get here."

"I know," she said, and the sadness threaded through her words made a pang run through him, unfamiliar, unwanted, unbalancing. Jeremiah frowned, trying to shove the feelings away, and started cutting pieces of integument to fit over Loni's last wounds.

It was late afternoon when Jeremiah woke. Finishing Loni's repairs had taken most of the night. When he rose from his bed, Shim told him that he still had the important message from New Day Environmental, along with a new one from the Historical Zone Governing Board. New Day, or Loni's old owners, had already run to his bosses. Ignoring them, he dressed and went looking for her.

The droid was still in his workshop, plugged in and charging up. But there was a little pile of things next to her, freshly made by the fabricator. More dresses, sun hats, parasols, boots, a backpack. He looked at them, and when he looked back at Loni, she had opened her clear lids.

"I am afraid I have taken advantage of your hospitality again," she said. "I suppose this is a circumstance where I am asking forgiveness, instead of permission."

"You're going." There was a pang behind those words, unfamiliar and unwanted, and Jeremiah thought about turning and going back to bed. She would probably be gone when he got back up tomorrow. But tempting as it was, he couldn't. "I purchased a new security suite for Shim. The scavengers won't be able to sneak by next time. We'll have warning. I can keep you safe. Safer than out there."

"Safe from scavengers, but not legal proceedings," Loni said.

"I can talk to them," he said. "Prove you're sentient."

"Prove I'm human?" she asked, head tilting.

He shrugged. "Same difference."

"No," Loni said. "No, it's not." She unplugged herself and wound up her charging cord, tucking it away and sealing her port back up behind her clear, freshly repaired integument. "Jeremiah Molina. I cannot express how indebted I am to you. You have saved my life twice and given me a place to rest and think for a time. A service so valuable it might count as a third lifesaving rescue. And you have been my friend, my first friend, ever. I will always be grateful for all of that and hold you dear in my heart. But I cannot stay with you. Not because of the danger to me, not because of the danger to you, though both of those weigh on my decision. I cannot stay because you cannot, will not, acknowledge the most important thing about me. That I am a person, not a thing."

"I know what you are," Jeremiah said gruffly, looking away from her.

"I think you do," she said, her voice soft but certain. "But you can't acknowledge it. Not really. You can't let me be human, Jeremiah, because you can't stand other people, their complexities, their confusions, their needs. That's why you left them and came to this place, to take care of things, because they are simple and uncomplaining and can be fixed and stay fixed. People aren't like that. *I'm* not like that, no matter how much you might like to think I am." She got up from the table and began to put her new belongings into the pack. "You wish I was because, despite how unbalancing everyone else is, you are still human, and after all these years out in the middle of this sea of grass, you are lonely. You want companionship, but you hate complication. An unbalanced equation, unsolvable. Until you met me and imagined that I might be the answer."

"I'm not lonely!" Jeremiah snapped, suddenly angry. Loni looked at him, ears pricked, as she shut her backpack. "Fine, you're human, is that what you want to hear? A stupid human, as frustrating as all the other fools out there!"

"Then why didn't you get rid of me when I showed up, like the other roamers?" Loni asked.

"Because!" he said. "There was just one of you! And . . . " And she had fur and a tail and coolant tubes—he shut his mouth.

"Because you didn't see a person in need," she said. "So you helped me. If you had seen another human, you would have gotten rid of me." Loni shrugged the backpack on. "People are cruel to each other for many reasons, but one of them is self-defense. We don't want to be entangled in the unsolvable problems of others when we already have so many of our own. So we ignore them and ignore the pain that doing so causes." She sighed, pulling in air just to let it out, to make that human sound of frustration. "You drove out the roamers because you saw in them a reflection of yourself, and your issues. You let me stay, because you saw a reflection of Kearney, something you could fix." Loni dropped her new boots to the floor and stepped into them. "But I'm not a broken clock, a stuck window, a mower with dull blades. I'm human, Jeremiah, and some of the things that make me broken make me *me*, and they can't be, shouldn't be, fixed."

It was stupid, Jeremiah thought. Being broken was messy, was painful, was wrong, and . . . He turned away, staring unseeing at his workshop, neat and organized, stuffed with tools, each one in their place. "I like fixing things."

"You do," she said. "But I'm not a thing."

He heard her boots against the floor, her claws on the door handle, the low squeak of hinges that needed oil. "Wait," he said. He went to the bins on one side of the room, pulling out the components he wanted, then turned. She stood in the door, dressed in her hat and boots and dress, backpack slung over her shoulder, like a character from a children's book, Ms. Otter goes on an Adventure, except her fur was gone, and her skin was clear, and she was all myofiber bundles and coolant tubes and teeth and eyes, an otter flayed into something alien, artificial, monstrous but elegant.

"This is a backup battery and a solar charging system," he said, holding out the components. "They'll make your pack heavy, but with them you'll be self-sufficient for . . . " He shrugged. Pasu Mastercraft did good work. "Years, probably. If you stay away from the buffalo."

She walked back and let him load the things into her pack. When he was done, she looked up at him with her wide brown eyes. "Thank you, Jeremiah. Thank you for everything." Then she reached out and rested her small, clawed hand on his. "It's OK to want to fix things. And it's OK to be frustrated when you can't. Especially when what you can't fix is yourself."

Then she took her hand away, and the tap of her boots disappeared as she left the workshop and headed out into the night, the moon stretching her thin shadow out across the streets of Kearney as she walked away from him and into the world.

ABOUT THE AUTHOR

Gary Kloster is a writer, a librarian, a martial arts instructor, and stay-at-home father. Sometimes all in the same day, but seldom all at the same time. He lives in the midwest of the United States, surrounded by corn and beset by cats. His stories have appeared in *Analog, Clarkesworld, Escape Pod, Fantasy Magazine,* and many others. He has also written a number of books for the Warhammer 40K and Age of Sigmar universes.

Serpent Carriers

K.A. TERYNA, TRANSLATED BY ALEX SHVARTSMAN

Old people are of little use, but on occasion, they know stories and are skilled at telling them. Jorge, an old man with a face wrinkled and cracked like last year's berry, kept his stories to himself.

As she looked at him from afar, Rioja imagined how stories accumulated within Jorge, how they roiled and mixed and quarreled. There was probably an ever-present and tremendous tumult within his head. Jorge spent his nights with the shepherds: He sat hunched over, just outside the range of the light cast by the fire, and smoked his pipe in silence. He listened to others but told no stories of his own. The shepherds didn't like Jorge but didn't dare chase him away. When Jorge approached the fire, the shepherds exchanged glances and frowned but still offered him a helping of broth in a rusty mug. You never knew when old people might be ready to die, and when they're ready, what their last word will be, and whether that last word will be about you. And whether it will be a Word.

It had been a long time since Words existed on Ilion; only their descriptions were passed from father to son, like a grandfather's snuffbox in a city devoid of tobacco. But the memory of Words continued to instill a vague unease. People recalling them would glance disapprovingly at the sky with its two moons; the sky where Words used to come from, along with Meteor Birds and news of the greater world. Over many quiet years, Words became a legend, which only children were foolhardy enough to repeat since their souls weren't yet encased in the crust of quietude.

Fall had always been the time to gather supplies. To store extra quantities of berries, stories, and warmth. Even Rioja's decrepit yak, who disliked cities and well-trodden shepherd paths, sought out the company of his kind in the fall.

All the cities Rioja and her yak encountered on their journey were alike: the old world waned in the embrace of Ilion's bountiful nature;

Archaic and Benzel plants covered the walls of houses; yaks wandered the wide boulevards and spacious squares; and unflappable shepherds smoked in the shadows of crumbling walls.

Rioja would leave her yak to graze on the outskirts and wander in places where it couldn't pass: the labyrinths of narrow streets in the heart of the city. She wasn't looking for anything specific but tried to find purpose in what she saw. At times, she thought that purpose was hidden in the rays of light broken by the city skyline, odd and—for some reason—very cheerful. She'd walk in the shade of the old streets, turn the corner, and encounter perfection. She'd suddenly realize those who came before had walked these streets in the same way for hundreds and thousands of years.

The farm towers rose in the east, impressive even at a great distance. Shepherds disliked the eastern wind and were suspicious of any person from the east. Rioja came from the west and could've told them that the farms were the same everywhere, that western farms were no better than the eastern ones. But she remained silent and hid her wrists and palms within long sleeves.

The fall in southern Ilion was soft and golden. As she gazed at the carpet of leaves, Rioja thought that perhaps they held purpose. Or perhaps it was in the crunching sound, loud enough to spread across empty streets, when she waded knee-deep in those leaves. At times, she saw the old Jorge in the distance—snoozing on the bench under the broken clock in front of the train station building.

She had explored the entire city, and it was time to move on, but Rioja hesitated. She was curious about Jorge. She wanted a closer look. Either sensing her curiosity or obeying the will of the fall, Jorge became restless and perturbed. It seemed as though he was not a single person but two or three or a whole dozen. At times, he didn't seem like a person at all.

Each night, he sat closer and closer to the fire and seemed to fight against the urge to tell a story in response to the heavy-handed shepherd yarns about love, inheritance, and family squabbles. Jorge opened his mouth and closed it again, and Rioja thought he must be experiencing the pain of a vase that had cracked but hadn't yet shattered.

When Rioja had nearly decided it was time to move on, the old man began to speak.

The stories punched a hole in his silence and emerged, flowing from his eyes like bitter tears, emanating through his trembling fingers, tumbling through the sounds of his hoarse voice unaccustomed to lengthy conversations.

His first story was about a boy.

The boy had trouble sleeping; whenever he closed his eyes, he thought he was being stalked by words.

The boy's father was a space pilot—that's what his mother and grandmother had told him. But the boy didn't listen to the words and instead listened to the underlying meaning. And the meaning was this: Father had gone away, leaving the boy and his mom behind.

Words masqueraded their meaning like dilapidated cardboard sets at the edge of the roiling abyss. Sometimes it would seem that the slightest gust of wind from the greater world would be enough to crumble these sets into dust. But Mother and Grandmother would, on occasion, touch up the cardboard sets so that the carcass of their worldview could remain unchanged: somewhere out there, a great war was raging, and Father was doing his duty, destroying the enemies of the Empire. Which also made them the enemies of all things righteous and just.

The boy saw words for what they were: unpleasant monsters who devoured meaning. Words buzzed everywhere like swarms of insects. Sometimes the boy wanted to stomp upon them, and sometimes he wanted to study them.

The boy imagined meaning to also be a living creature. A small, skittish, slippery thing akin to a Yurgian birchcat with big yellow saucers for eyes. The boy sometimes thought how nice it would be if he could learn to weave special traps that could capture meaning and then domesticate it so it could point with its wet, cold nose toward the truth.

The words about war and Empire were bark beetles. They deftly bored tunnels straight through people's heads.

Once a year, the family gathered around the table to celebrate Father's birthday, but in lieu of the guest of honor, only a holographic portrait of a young space pilot emitted by a fragile old projector was present. Father's stern and demanding gaze always found the boy, who thought the sharp blade of that gaze would cut open his skull at any moment, scoop out every seditious thought, then count and catalog them.

Only Aunt Luisa would speak the truth about the words. She was a petite old woman whose scarred palms and wrists betrayed her past on a farm. Luisa was a loner; the city folk, even her relatives, avoided her. Strange words buzzed about her like annoying gnats. People said that Luisa was a digital witch who had a farm device with hammers and matrices in her head instead of a human brain. People said that the farms sent their spies into cities in order to steal children. That the birds were among the farm spies. The boy recalled how, one year, it was considered the height of bravery to kill every pigeon one saw. The birds on Ilion were brightly colored and small. The boy was not afraid of them, but he hid from the large Meteor Birds, who truly were spies—spies for the Empire.

When the Meteor Birds would fly by, children went to meet them at the city spaceport in the hope that their fathers and mothers had returned. It was rare for parents to return. Rumor had it that the Empire was dead, but its war continued to masticate people as it always had, and only rarely spat one out of its foul mouth. Instead of their parents, the children received Words. Words fluttered in their heads like evil hatchlings, demanding attention and obedience. Words called them to war, to distant places under the banner of the Empire. The children who were too young for such words lay dry and hot like the Eastern stone lizards. Some died, others survived, and the Imperial Words no longer threatened their will. The Words took captive the older ones, who were no longer kids. The teenagers waited for the Meteor Birds and rode them into the maw of war. Some mothers locked up their sons and daughters in their basements until the acute phase of the infection passed. The children scraped their hands raw against the walls, overcome with love for the Empire and their distant ancestral motherland. Words made them crafty in the way drugs do. Children would convince their mothers that the danger had passed and then leave Ilion at the first opportunity.

Whenever the Meteor Birds flew by, the boy remained home. He gazed from afar at their predatory metallic silhouettes and their fanged beaks, designed to chew up singularities; at their powerful armor capable of withstanding fire and ice and time. Once, Mother had claimed that Father's failure to return was the boy's fault. That he wasn't coming back because the boy wasn't going out to greet him. The boy vaguely realized the logical fallacies inherent in such a theory, but the accusation stung painfully, anyway.

Aunt Luisa said that the war had ended a long time ago. But the Words continued to function, and each time someone left, they found somebody to fight against out in the greater world. Imperial Words hunted the free people of Ilion and deprived them of their peace of mind. The boy kept wondering what the Words might do with that peace. Perhaps, he thought, they collected it in a huge cave and pressed it into bars, preserved against some future need.

The boy thought that if he were to find this cave, there would be enough peace stored there to permanently drown out all seedlings of war and all echoes of the dead Empire.

Aunt Luisa said the Imperial Words were getting weaker with every passing year—all except the Prime Word.

The boy imagined the Prime Word to be very long and complicated. Insidiocontagious. In the boy's imagination, the Prime Word had thousands of hooked teeth, a maw with a sharp, venomous tongue, and an ingratiating, soothing voice. The boy saw it lurking under the bed, in a dark basement he had to enter, in the eyes of every stranger.

Aunt Luisa told him that the Prime Word had traveled the world for many centuries, ever since it had broken free from the imperial laboratories. The Prime Word seeks out special people and turns them into Serpent Carriers, who contain thousands of human lives within their own. The Prime Word encircles the special person, its chosen one, like a serpent. This person follows the path laid out by the serpent and carries that serpent with them.

The Prime Word kills regular people. It moves from person to person at the moment of death, and it knows no other way. Aunt Luisa explained that the only reason the Prime Word hasn't taken over the world is because almost everyone out there is a regular person.

But the person selected by the Serpent Word lives the lives of dozens or even hundreds of people. They gain unimaginable powers. It is said some knew how to devour stars, and others could talk to fish. Some became heroes of legend, others yet had been referred to as gods.

The boy couldn't decide whether he'd rather be one of the regular people who would die like everyone else or if he'd rather be a special person who could become a god. And whether he ever wanted to meet the Prime Word and find out in the first place.

Aunt Luisa would stroke his hair with cool fingers and vocalize, her voice shifting up and down the register. The boy followed it like a kitten tracking a speck of sunlight and then fell asleep. Aunt Luisa's melody would persist in the dream, except it'd be the boy singing. He was a musician by the fire in a wasteland, playing a simple wooden pipe. In the dream, the words answered his call, stretched next to him like animals who only remained harmless for as long as he played well. The boy knew that there, beyond the range of the firelight, waited other Words—creatures made according to the drafts and laws of the Empire, carriers of war.

Far away from the fire, at the border of light and sound, nearly indistinguishable from the silence and the darkness, lurked the question seeded by Aunt Luisa and grown in the fertile soil of the boy's doubt: who are you—an ordinary mortal or a godlike hero?

• • •

Time is no river, as many people think. It isn't even a swarm of tiny invisible critters who devour human lives, as posited by a certain hermit who lived on an asteroid because he thought the treacherous invisible critters couldn't reach him there.

Time slithered into the boy's house along with the death of his mother. Perhaps Mother had spent too much time at the spaceport, and the cells of her body lost their will to live. Perhaps there was no lesson to the story, and Mother died because it was her time.

It turned out, Grandmother handled grief in a practical and dexterous manner. She didn't bow down to it, didn't invite it into her home, didn't offer it a comfortable place to stay. She quickly snapped the grief's neck as though it were a skinny chicken. She skinned it, baked it in the oven, and fed it to the neighbors for a repast.

Over the next three days, she sold all their city possessions, stained with the blood of bereavement and splashes of memory. She gathered all their savings and used them to buy a small, patched up, but still functional yak.

The boy sat in his room in the house that had been sold to strangers and refused to leave. He had no special love for this room and this city, and no fear of the wastelands. But the words that awaited him out there seemed far more dangerous outside the familiar walls.

Grandmother didn't know how to handle the boy, so she called Aunt Luisa. The latter said: The war is over, the words are weak—both the imperial ones woven out of specially crafted genes, and the typical Ilionian ones, crafted from letters and memories. Lead a quiet existence, keep the peace, honor your ancestors, and your life will be good. But the boy stubbornly remained silent. He thought all of this was a bitter lie, and that sweet lies did not exist. But Luisa backed up her statements with a gift: a glass pendant made out of an ampule. She'd had it for as long as the boy remembered.

The pendant came with a red graphite string and a backstory. The true value of any worthwhile thing comes from its backstory, and the backstory of the pendant was simple: Luisa and her brother—the boy's father—had inherited it from their mother. Before Luisa, the pendant was in her family's possession for six generations. The ampule hailed from the same imperial laboratories where they crafted word-viruses. It was a lucky lottery ticket some distant ancestor had earned for his long-forgotten achievements. It was said such an ampule would protect the wearer from the Word. Luisa didn't tell the boy how, many years ago, she'd offered his father to cast dice to determine who would get it. He'd refused with contempt, for he considered the ampule nothing more than a bauble and the family legend nothing more than a shepherd's tale. The power of such items often isn't in their contents but in the faith that we imbue into them.

There were a lot fewer words in the wastelands. The wastelands were ruled by silence, peace, and the yaks. Huge like the walking houses, yaks were also leftovers of the Empire. Some dared to consider them to be tamed technology. In reality, it was the yaks who had tamed the shepherds.

The yaks forged their own paths through the wastelands. The yaks loved old cities; the yaks hated the mycelium farms. They were scavengers, but this label didn't demean them. It was such a small term, and the yaks were so very big. The yaks followed the footsteps of receding civilization and devoured its remnants. In the past, the materials recycled by the yaks would've been delivered to warehouses, then sent back to the heart of the Empire. This was akin to the funeral rite for an ancient murderer, when the body of the decedent would be sent down the river, to his gods.

But the warehouses had fallen into disuse sooner than the cities of Ilion. Some had rapidly turned into farms, while others became yak food.

Unable to regurgitate the old civilization in the expected way, the yaks had used it to create. Their works stood everywhere along the yak paths: road markers and sculptures, the meaning of which was beyond any shepherd. At times, people had to wait patiently whenever inspiration would strike a yak, and it would set out to improve upon the works of its predecessors. For the yaks, art was a collective endeavor. Some argued that their behavior was akin to animals who marked territory along their path.

Sometimes, railroad tracks sprouted from yak sculptures, extended into the distance, and terminated somewhere far away. They were the sprouts of wild sedge, erupting from the seal of the Empire in the atomic hearts of the yaks. The boy thought that, one day, those pointless tracks would intertwine into something meaningful, and they'd gain a sentience of their own.

The boy shed his city fears, spread his metaphorical wings, and explored the plains. Predators waited for him there. Despite the prevalence of silence, there were some regular human words present, but not the imperial viruses. In the wide spaces of the wastelands, the boy grew bolder and learned how to handle them: he'd catch them in his palm, examine them, count the number of their paws, and set them free.

The yak slowly followed a route that was apparent only to itself. This symbolized life in general. The boy rode under the canopy on the yak's back and observed the world.

They would rest in the evenings, sometimes in the sea of grass, sometimes amidst the dead cities. The boy and his grandmother joined the other shepherds. The grandmother remained silent because she knew life, and the boy remained silent because he didn't. The shepherds leisurely shared their stories, and the boy caught those tales within the traps of his attention, mentally disassembled and sorted the words, as if they were peas and lentils, upon the table of his imagination.

The time flowed differently in the plains—it was viscous and somewhat bitter. It was not measured by the Meteor Birds, even though the boy sometimes saw their trails up in the sky. The yaks avoided living cities, and the birds didn't land in the dead ones.

Grandmother died peacefully in the quiet bliss of the simple life. The boy buried her according to the rites of the plains: the yak and its atomic engine accepted all offerings. Soon after, the news arrived via shepherd post—person-to-person—of Aunt Luisa's death. The boy built a funeral cairn in her memory, in the place where the news caught up to him. Months later, this cairn turned into a sculpture. In this manner, the boy became a cocreator to the yak tribe.

Otherwise, life went on unchanged: a series of landscapes, evening fires, and the shadows of words basking by the flames. It was almost exactly how the boy had imagined it as a child. Somewhere outside the light of the fire, the largest shadow always waited. It was the shadow of the question, of whether the boy was a great man or a regular one. What would happen if he ever encountered the Prime Word? The boy learned not to look in the shadow's direction.

The boy celebrated his coming of age in the shepherd style: he cut off the childhood braid that had been woven by his mother. Soon, he got married. The boy didn't understand love; it was yet another treacherous word to him. But he well understood custom and peace, and his wife valued his quietude.

It was when his daughter was born that the boy felt the words disappear for the first time. They were absent within and without, and even the shadow of the question planted by Aunt Luisa had disappeared when the boy held his daughter for the first time. In that moment, there was no room for words or questions or shadows, because if there's such a thing in this world as perfection, it is hidden within the feeling of continuation of oneself. The boy removed Luisa's pendant from around his neck and placed it around his daughter's.

Benzel leaves wilted and fell and grew afresh. Archaic plants dug their little claws deeper into the walls of ancient buildings, and heavy berries fell from them in autumn. The yak carried the boy and his family by routes known only to the yaks. These routes always passed through the fading cities. The yaks had a special sense and learned about the dying cities before the shepherds did.

One time, the yak brought them to the boy's hometown. The city was empty and dead, but it hadn't yet been covered by the dust of oblivion. The yaks wandered across it, grazing upon the tastiest walls and sidewalks.

The boy left his wife and daughter with the yak and wandered the streets of his hometown alone. He found his house without difficulty, and the window he once used to watch city life; to watch boys and girls attracted by loudspeaker announcements and clouds severed by trails, rushing to board the trams toward the spaceport.

At one point, every city in Ilion had had a spaceport. Salt had been cheap then, and during the peak of the Ilion civilization, every city had strived to hang a platform for feeding Meteor Birds. It was akin to a dream catcher, more symbolic than practical. Back when the warehouses still functioned and the logistics hadn't yet broken down into thousands of tiny shreds, these feeders were filled with sky salt.

The spaceports were similar to the yaks in this cultural ouroboros. In order to service the birds that had become nearly mythological by then, they needed to remain close to the clouds, which required salt. There were fewer and fewer cities as the yaks devoured them. But the spaceports remained, like the birdhouses in a burned-out forest, as the awkward testament to Ilion's cattle-like obedience. There was enough salt stored in their storerooms that a futile wait for the Meteor Birds could last decades or even centuries.

The boy followed the phantom crowd of his peers down the narrow streets, deeper into the heart of the city, where the birdhouse-spaceport hovered with a quiet hum. Surprisingly, the gravity tram designed to carry people between the ground and the sky still functioned. The tram greeted the boy with a rusty *ding*, and the boy stepped inside. As soon as the tram disembarked from the platform, the boy looked up at the approaching silhouette of the spaceport and saw the sky dissected by the unmistakable inverse trail of a Meteor Bird.

The Meteor Birds hadn't appeared for a really long time. The boy had nearly forgotten they even existed. The old fear shifted within his heart, swiped at his insides with its little claws. The boy made to clasp Aunt Luisa's pendant, only to recall that he had given it away to his daughter.

The tram ascended to its destination and hovered at the platform, trembling with pride as this was the first time in years that it'd had a passenger.

The Meteor Bird stood in the middle of the enormous platform, its silhouette dark and tempered by vacuum.

Behind him, the tram dinged, calling for passengers to take their seats. The boy glanced back at its cozy interior, illuminated by the evening lights. He suddenly recalled his mother's absurd accusation: that Father had never returned only because the boy was not waiting for him. Mother was long gone, her grave covered by thick Benzel leaves, but Aunt Luisa also wasn't there and could not explain to the boy the futility of arguing with the dead.

The boy walked toward the bird. As if it were waiting just for that, a door opened in the bird's chest, revealing a ramp and a sole person standing on it.

The boy studied the space pilot's silhouette, seeking out details he'd seen in the hologram portrait. The man was old; had the boy met him among the shepherds or at one of the plain fairs, he'd walk right by without a second glance. The boy realized that he wouldn't have been able to tell his father apart from any Ilionian masticated by the Empire. He also realized that it didn't matter because this man was more than simply a man.

The boy saw letters and meanings intertwined into a single construct, heavy yet graceful. Having spent so much time studying the invisible forms of regular words, he couldn't miss the signs in the way the man walked, the way he held himself, the impatient twitch of his fingers, and his piercing, squinting gaze, that the man carried a different Word. Not the Prime Word, no, Luisa had been wrong about that. The Divine Word.

This is how friends and enemies recognize one another—a person akin to them in spirit whom they've never met before. Love and hatred don't happen at first sight. They're preceded by dreams and trepidations.

The Word also recognized the boy. He saw this in the eyes of the space pilot as they filled with tears. Tears trailed confusing paths down his cheeks, leaving red stains. From that chaos, letters were born along with the scent of salt and time, and the whisper foretelling a grandiose future. The shadow stepped within the circle of the boy's inner light, illuminated by his sharpened attention. The question once seeded by Luisa had been finally watered by the rain of blood, and the boy took a step toward the Serpent Carrier.

Jorge stopped talking, and no one dared interrupt the silence. Everyone focused on their thoughts as the old man's story bloomed within them like the blue lily flower. Grim fairy-tales from the shepherds' childhoods—awkward but pretty ethnographic monsters that mutated like viruses as they were transferred from person to person—rumbled sleepily within their memories.

Rioja thought about the boy and the question that had lured him into the Meteor Bird's trap. At the far edge of her consciousness, she noted the movement of shadows beyond the circle of light birthed by the fire. She didn't have to look closer; she knew it was that same question, and now it examined her with patience, trepidation, and a touch of sarcasm. Was this question the thing she'd been seeking for so long? Was it meaning?

Jorge said nothing as he drank his broth and gazed at the quiet shepherds from under his thick eyebrows. Somewhere at the borders of the dead city, the yaks made noise, whistled, and talked.

The old man set his bowl aside and resumed talking.

Emancipation Day

The second story was about a girl.

The girl had lived on a farm for almost as long as she could remember.

Almost the entirety of her memory was the comforting, endless, shared ocean, but somewhere in the furthest reaches of her physical brain, in the plexuses of rebel neutrons, hid the remnants of her personal memories.

Sometimes they snuck into the edges of her "we."

The portrait of her grandfather as a young man was displayed among the icons with a little ion candle placed in front of it. The shape of her mother, hunched over her sewing; a thimble, needles stuck into a bunny-shaped pillow. The strained snoring of a yak.

Personal memories were predatory shadows hovering over the pacific surface of timelessness. They beckoned the girl in order to grab her and snatch her from the ocean's embrace. Near the surface, when her heart raced in terror, the girl knew it: the Emancipation Day was nigh. These were the signs of time invading the cozy world of timeless "we."

The knowledge of Emancipation Day was part of the unity between the girl and the farm. The knowledge that it was permissible to leave. To wait for day zero of the cycle, when the farm would accept new workers, and take a step away, a step out. This knowledge was not comforting. If anything, it was the opposite. From the moment the girl became part of the farm, Emancipation Day became a sort of threat, a reminder that even the endless ocean of timeless "we" had a border. How sweet it was to forget that!

It was impossible not to notice the approach of Emancipation Day. First, memory peeled away, then the girl began to feel the self and the flow of time, and to separate the "I" from the "we" and days from timelessness.

The days were troublous but also happy. This is simple: It's impossible to feel happiness while situated inside of it. Emancipation Day, with its ghosts of the past and thorny time, forced the girl to almost leave the ocean, to step into the shallowest of waters, but also allowed her the opportunity to know it, to desire a return, to anticipate the descent.

The approach of Emancipation Day also brought physical feelings. The girl vaguely recalled that they were varied and included some pleasant ones. But against the background of the receding timeless "we," all her physical body felt was pain.

Pain of awakening and pain of sunlight. Pain of hunger and pain of satiation. Pain of exhaustion and pain of repose.

All that was left to her was to return to the ocean in her thoughts, to reach for it with her sole remaining consciousness, to try and understand the incomprehensible. To dream of a quick return while struggling through the routine of existence on the farm.

This existence was boring and meaningless. It was as though the girl who occupied the vast whirling world of adventure and euphoria peeked through the keyhole at the children of shepherds playing at dolls made from sticks and rocks.

Even in advance of Emancipation Day, the girl didn't fully return to her physical body but rather watched herself, as if from a distance, without distinguishing between her own body and the bodies of thousands of other workers on the farm.

Emancipation Day came and went, and nothing changed. Slowly, as if plunging into salt water, the girl returned to the timeless "we."

In its mercy, the ocean never suddenly changed its dimensions. The fragile consciousness of an individual is incapable of comprehending a rapid transition from four dimensions to twenty-four. From "I" to "we." Therefore, a melody was added first. It was pure and simple, like the first snow in the morning. The sound became a dimension, splitting into two voices, then into eight. At first, these voices sounded external and strange, then the girl began to sing herself, to weave her thread into the communal strand. Another step, and she became the voices, all of them at once. Gradually, a grandiose landscape of subtemporal depths emerged from the darkness: statistical mountain peaks and chasms, tornadoes of white noise, probabilistic monsters and fish.

The girl no longer existed there. She was fully woven into the fabric of statistics, not as a patch over a hole but dissolving the sparks of her mind across the canvas and letting waves of probabilistic pleasure wash through her.

This moment was worth waiting for—while you were still enough of an individual to feel the joy and experience this beauty somewhat from the outside—it was worth living through Emancipation Day, time after time.

It was like riding the wave: first all the way up to the sky, wary of slamming against its crystal, then down, to the depths.

But once, there was no more "down." The sky approached, and the girl slammed against it at full speed. The force of impact broke the girl into the tiniest shards, which immediately disappeared—all except the last minuscule one. The girl was left in the absolute freezing solitude of her primitive mind and had no one to share it with.

She'd been disconnected.

There was no concept of death in the timeless "we," just like there had been no individualistic "I."

Death was the first thing the girl remembered having emerged from the saltwater timelessness. That's what she thought: *we've died.*

The girl opened her eyes. Her eyes had opened millions of times in the years spent at the farm, but this was the first time she'd opened them herself, consciously. The palette of Emancipation Day, the pain in every neuron, collapsed upon her in all of its monotony. The light from the distant sky, reflected a thousand times by leaves and mirrors, cut her with stinging shards of pure pain. Her skin burned and itched. The girl had so much skin. There was so much of the girl, and also, infinitely little. The girl stared at the green labyrinth in the atrium above her, at the blue sky peeking through vegetation and the sunspots. She stared and didn't want to see.

There was no ocean. The meaning was gone.

The place where the girl's body had been disconnected was familiar to her. The girl's body knew the entire farm. Her legs had been everywhere, her hands had repaired, plowed, fertilized, pruned, cleaned, tuned, buried, dug up, sowed, washed, pollinated—but in the thousands, hundreds of thousands, millions of those moments the girl's consciousness was elsewhere—in the beautiful multidimensional reality of the timeless "we." Her body knew every square meter of the farm, but her mind recalled only one place: the one where, many years ago, she'd been connected to the farm.

And now she was back in that place.

Recognition was not a pleasant feeling. Recognition was an Ilion yak someone had tied the girl to, and now the yak was picking up speed, heading in the direction only it knew, dragging the girl on the ground behind it.

Time collapsed upon her with all its weight. For many years, the ocean had protected her from time, as it protected all of its children. There was the internal world—consciousness that melded in infinity with the farm ecosystem, with every flower and root, with the mycelium spread throughout the farm. And there were the external—bodies, hands, fingers, doors, petals, fertilizer, hyphae, faces, sterilization chambers, stalks, microclimate systems, solar panels—that were only the carcass, the foundation, the walls surrounding the world. The girl became a brick in the fence, and this brick was superfluous. The time bore down on her, pressed her, and stretched her out. The time shook her with its trickster hands. The time cackled. The time lashed at the farm walls with wind and creaked mournfully.

Her consciousness was unused to existing, and the girl felt like the moments of her life were mixed and laid out on the table at random: the past mixed with the present, and in some fragments, the girl thought she caught glimpses of the future.

The girl closed her eyes.

The thread had always been there. A thin carmine-red graphite cord—its color hadn't faded over the years—held a small transparent ampule the size of a baby's finger. When Mom bent down, the ampule hung loose; when she straightened up, the ampule rested at her chest.

Mom sewed, she was always sewing or stitching or patching or knitting something. Her hands knew no rest. It was night, and the atomic heart of a yak rustled quietly. Mom whispered an old fairy-tale, the yak listened, and the shell moved steadily up and down, the thread approached and receded. Receded and ran, ran somewhere into darkness.

Knock knock. Hiss hiss. The thread disappeared, replaced with sound.

The girl closed her eyes.

Strange hands laid her down upon the bed of mycelium. The hyphae unraveled beneath her to interlock around her wrists, ankles, and neck. It smelled damp. She had no strength to resist; hunger was devouring her from within. The digital witch had hardly fed her in recent days, as they traversed the autumnal wasteland, farther and farther from the yak, from Mom, from the evening fire.

The children were best suited; their psyches only seemed tender at first glance. The mighty jaws of the child's psyche would mercilessly chew through any new input, the claws would dig into the strangest society, the joints would twist and adapt, the heart would learn a new rhythm. This is why the farms always valued children.

If she slowed down a lot, she could hear the movement of the hyphae. Another sound cut through into her consciousness: it was rough, alarming, intermittent.

The girl closed her eyes.

Manna grew everywhere; it was white, greasy, and soft. Tenacious. Reach for it with your eyes closed, and your fingers will recognize it, and the feeding reflex will kick in.

Manna is practical. Convenient for a quick and nutritious feeding of workers. Manna is part of the ecosystem. The girl squinted and allowed her hands to stuff her mouth with crumbling berries.

For a brief moment, the taste of manna did the impossible: through recognition and physiological satisfaction, via the labyrinths of mutilated memory, it returned her into the ocean, brought her into the epicenter of the statistical storm. Where there was no light or darkness. Where the landscape is sewn out of possibilities. Where one breathed in chaos and breathed out silence. In that was joy, and meaning, and the juices of life.

For a brief moment, the consciousness and the body separated again and separately gave in to the power of the ocean, the farm, the mycelium. It was wonderful not to think, not to know, not to seek, but simply to exist.

But the moment had passed. The storm, the statistic, the possibilities, the music, all remained behind, somewhere far among the filaments of hyphae, the enormous fungal network permeating the farm. The girl was here. So was the sound. Creaky and viscous like jam made from late-blooming berries.

The girl closed her eyes.

There was no mycelium where the girl lay. It retreated as if she were poisonous. Her body convulsed, and people walked by indifferently. Not people, but workers. Emancipation Day had just passed, and the new workers—children and teenagers—had already connected to the network. Mycelium worked fast. Their eyes were vacant, and the girl felt nauseous. Out of envy, she thought.

A dead old man lay next to her. He was among the people who had come to give themselves over to the farm but were rejected. Every time, when she opened her eyes, the girl turned to look at him and found his profile somehow comforting.

When three workers came to remove his body, she got up on her knees and then staggered to her full height. The workers shied away from her in the same manner as the hyphae.

The girl wasn't sure why she wasn't letting them take the old man's body. Perhaps she'd grown used to him. Perhaps he was the only person here toward whom she didn't feel envious. Then she forgot all about him as a huge and very important thought displaced everything else: she had to survive until the next Emancipation Day. Not to give up. To stay.

The girl knew that the mycelium was still watching her, she felt its cool, damn attention. But the sound wouldn't let her focus on it—a foreign, thick, crunchy autumnal sound, like that of the leaves under someone's foot.

The girl closed her eyes.

Some people arrived on their own—the desperate, the ones desirous of oblivion, seeking an external force that would make all decisions for them, yearning for euphoria. Others were brought by the ones called digital witches. Disconnected from the mycelium, too old to return, too weak to forget. They procured children for the mycelium, either in hopes of praise and the fleeting attention of the ocean, or for the benefit of the children themselves.

The girl tried to remember what she'd felt when the mycelium took her. The light but commanding touch of the hyphae. The sound of blood in her ears. The scent of dampness, still unfamiliar, still alien. If she were to recall and repeat everything in the proper order, perhaps the mycelium would accept her again?

But the creaking sound had crept in here too, into this almost comforting thought. Somewhat hoarse and impudent. It sounded like—what?

The girl closed her eyes.

There was the back of a worker's head in front of her. Long, tangled hair. A shirt that had half-rotted on the worker's body and would soon disintegrate. There was no use for a shirt on a farm. The body under the shirt was stained with dirt and covered with bruises. Mycelium didn't care what one looked like. It accepted people as they were. The worker emptied the containers and placed them into a receptacle of the washing machine. The girl diligently imitated this.

The girl decided: she simply needed to interject herself into the process, to ape the others, the happy, the connected. To demonstrate her suitability. To prove her meaningfulness.

The girl didn't have much faith in her suitability or meaningfulness. But what if—if—mycelium simply confused her with one of the connected? And took her home.

She was pushed aside, removed, driven away. Without violence or threats or physical contact, but with the same tough steadfastness that she'd experienced from the other worker levels. Mycelium did not accept her.

The girl closed her eyes.

The girl hugged the old man's corpse and whispered something. She couldn't parse out what it was herself. The spark of consciousness snatched a moment from the darkness, without explanation of context. What came before? What would come after? The girl could only audit her feelings: the hunger inside of her; a hole where meaning used to be; an enmity toward the workers; tenderness toward the dead old man; an emptiness where something long forgotten used to reside; the sound that ached like an old wound and stung like a fresh scratch.

She wanted to cry but didn't know how. So she listened as a huge, bitter, and slimy lump swelled in her chest. It would displace her heart, fill her up, tear her, and maybe the entire farm, to shreds. Drown her in bitterness and tears.

The girl closed her eyes.

The wasteland in autumn was colored in turquoise and gold. The sun descended on the horizon, yielding to other celestial bodies: Wolf and Yurga, eternal rivals, eternal guardians of the night. The digital witch preferred to travel at night.

The birds that had served the witch faithfully in the nearly lifeless city were now dead and long since eaten. She had twisted their necks in a practiced, indifferent motion of her hand.

Now she held a girl with that hand, and the girl had to hurry to keep up with her sweeping gait. The digital witch resembled a bird herself; her movements appeared instinctive and subordinate to some unseen magnet. Inside of her lurked ammonites and ancient bones, dried seaweed and the desert—all in the place where the ocean of meanings should've been. Whispers hid in her eyes. It was crucial not to look at it directly and not to listen to it. The whisper wanted to wake the girl up. To keep her away from the mycelium. This couldn't be allowed.

The girl closed her eyes.

The girl turned her head and looked at the man next to her. He was no longer young and had the dark skin of a shepherd, a wrinkled face, and strands of gray hair. An old man. He would die soon, the girl thought indifferently. When mycelium accepted old people in its embrace, it was almost always a path toward death. The old people and the mycelium were both fine with that. Perhaps the old people's souls would become probabilistic storms or peaks of statistical mountains. A wonderful fate.

All around her were the new children of mycelium. She was the only stranger. She, and that irritatingly familiar sound. It came from somewhere outside, far away. And also, as if from within.

The girl closed her eyes.

She threw up manna and bile, and also meanings, words, and letters. The problem wasn't manna, it was the people around her. Their eyes were open, but they didn't see. Hyphae spread across the ground, wrapping their ankles. Hyphae stretched upward along the walls, embracing their wrists. The eyes were empty.

They didn't look at the girl, and didn't see her, but gave her a wide berth as though she were a carrier of mycophagous nematodes. She detested the way their faces varied, but detested even more how they were the same. The faces were unpleasant to her: languid masks of pale-blue skin. It was sickening to know that inside the storm, inside the huge, beautiful ocean of the timeless "we," she had been one with them. It was sickening to know that even now, her appearance was little different from theirs.

The old man beside her did not revolt her, perhaps because he was dead. The girl was surprised to find she was no longer indifferent to the old man's death. The sound that thoroughly entwined itself into her background also wasn't indifferent. As if the sound could feel or mourn. To cry for the old man.

The girl closed her eyes.

The girl stood at the roof's edge. Farms always occupied tall freestanding buildings, often at the top of a hill. There were no cities or tiny satellite settlements nearby. Only the solitary sun giant of a farm. Shepherds and yaks avoided it. There was something ancient and Abrahamic in this.

Her mind had nearly cleared, and time had settled. Occasionally, memories tossed her onto a carousel, but they resembled actual memories more and more; the girl no longer forgot where she was; she heard, saw, and felt the present. Only her thoughts reached back into the past.

The girl thought about the approaching Emancipation Day with calm detachment. The tingling in her fingers, wrists, and ankles promised that all would be well. She managed. The wait was over. Mycelium would forgive her and take her back, would allow her to give herself over to the communal piggy bank of human souls experiencing infinite statistical orgasms in the dimension of fungal joy.

The sound that stalked her in this limbo had reappeared. Sometimes it was nearly inaudible, sometimes it crescendoed, vibrated, permeated through skin. The chill of winter air and the coolness of metal under her soles and palms. The steady hum of ion nozzles, the trembling of a vast mechanical body, the smell of a coolant.

The sound was becoming clearer. The girl looked down and suddenly remembered: that was why she was here. To look down.

The sound peeled off, separated from her memories. The memories were somewhere over there. She was here. The sound was here too. It gained form and color. The form was a thread. The color was red.

The girl looked down and saw something she could describe but couldn't yet name. But the red thread was in her hand, and it led into darkness. The girl recalled a face.

The wastelands in the south are red-brown and wrinkled. As if Yagel moss played all night long under the cover of earth, and in the morning, the owner was too lazy to make up the bed.

A small town—a village rather—hid among those wrinkles. A dozen homes and a road paved orange. The yak kept away—the village wasn't sufficiently dead. The yak did not build its structures in places like this. It was very pleasant to watch the yak build. The girl thought it reminded her of poetry.

Sometimes poets gathered around the shepherds' fire. Poetry was reliable merchandise, and the poets were valued. Some poets construct their creations out of words. But there are others who wove together threads of meaning from beetles, birdsong, the movement of clouds, breaths, scents, and rustles.

The yak was also a poet. Its letters—tiny disposable drones—still smelled like the atoms of the old civilization. Whenever the yak was building, the girl wandered among the swarm of yak's letters, caught them one at a time, examined them, and let them free. Sometimes she lost a few. The yak didn't mind. Apparently, its improvisation accounted for her awkward participation.

That day, the yak wasn't building anything. It stood there, half-asleep and boring, while Mom examined its nodes and nozzles, checked the hermetic seals, cleaned the filters, and changed the oil, the coolant, and the ion batteries.

The girl traversed the edge of the village but didn't wander too far. She was a reasonable and obedient girl. Only once did she take the wrong turn: to watch the funny mating dance of sparrows in the dust.

There, beyond the corner, a digital witch with an ammonite stare and birds resting on her head and shoulders waited for her. The girl didn't manage to escape.

Run. Run. Run. Memory. It's only a memory.

The girl didn't close her eyes. Because the most important thing at that moment was to remain in the present. To hold on to the thread and to run, run down . . .

. . . down the staircase, floor by floor, holding on tight to the thread with her hands, her teeth, her entire consciousness. To remain in this moment, to make it last. Not to fall into the past or the future or the might-have-been. Not to surrender to the carousel of memories that had already claimed countless moments and insights.

The girl looked around just enough to keep going toward her destination. Her attention was needed elsewhere—to remember, to constantly remember the meaning of the sound she was hearing, why she was holding on to the thread, where she was going.

She kept running into the farm workers who had squeamishly parted before her. They moved awkwardly, uncertainly, in pairs or trios or quads, as if carrying out an unfamiliar routine. Too awkward. Deliberately awkward. The girl walked around them, slid past them, ducked underneath them. She pushed them out of her way. And she ran.

Wasn't that how Emancipation Day worked? Mycelium loosened its grip only to grasp on tighter. Mycelium never lets anyone go. If anyone managed to leave the farm forever, irrevocably, without paying a tribute in children—that was an accident, a statistical error. Mycelium thought in statistics, which, in turn, ignored people. Alone, you were nothing. A zero or a one, but more likely a zero. Irrelevant like a single spore whose life or death is unnoticeable from cyclopean heights. But while you were here, mycelium would do everything to make you stay.

The girl kept running until she reached the spot where the old man's corpse lay and where she'd spent several weeks.

He looked almost the same—as if he had died a moment ago or perhaps hadn't died at all but was sleeping. Mycelium knew how to accelerate decomposition when it was necessary, but it also knew how to halt it. Wasn't that the purpose it was created for by the imperial scientists? Eternal life is an eternal incentive for craven minds.

The girl knelt down before the pristine corpse, drowning in the multicolored mycelium. She let go of the imaginary thread, allowed it to dissolve in the darkness of memory, and leaned over the decedent. He had been dying while the girl was coming back to life. Not he, the girl realized, studying the decedent's face. She. She was dying. The decedent was a woman, and she wasn't even old but exhausted and devoured by grief. Stubborn. Patient. With a dark face burned by the Ilion sun. With hands that could do anything. With a red graphite thread on her neck, and a transparent ampule hanging from it made from medical grade glass.

The girl began to irreverently tear apart the hyphae cocoon.

Mom could do anything and negotiate with anyone—a yak, Yurga, or Wolf, even mycelium. Mom knew all the fairy-tales and told them better than anyone because she believed in them all.

There was this one fairy-tale about a girl who misbehaved and didn't obey her mother. Mother prohibited the girl from going into the undead cities, from feeding the birds, from looking up at Wolf. The girl didn't listen, and the digital witch stole her away, brought her to a farm, turned her into Yagel moss. But Mother never forgot the girl; she followed her. She wore out a hundred pairs of metal shoes, visited a hundred farms, talked to a hundred yaks. She hung a hundred digital witches at the crossroads, opened a hundred chests, and cut out a hundred witches' hearts. What could be described in a paragraph took years to accomplish, but eventually the mother reached the right farm, fell on her knees before mycelium, and begged it: "Take me and let my daughter go." Ash from a hundred witches' hearts was her burnt offering to the mycelium. And so, Emancipation Day came, and an exchange took place: a songbird turned into a little girl, sleepy and confused. The girl looked around and failed to recognize her mother because there was only a songbird in her place and no one to tell the girl this tale.

Things are simple in fairy-tales: one can talk to mycelium and even convince it. Reality is different. In reality, mycelium only lets a person go in order to bind to them even tighter. If it were so easy to leave mycelium behind, there would be no digital witches in the world.

The girl pondered this as she carried her mother's body through the farm's corridors. The girl had grown up in the years her mom spent searching, while Mother became diminished in death. The girl walked, and workers made way for her, but in a different manner than before. Reluctantly. With regret. The way a fat cat looks at the tail of the nearly eaten mouse that rolled under the baseboard.

The yak song is comprised of all sounds emitted by its systems. The beating of an atomic heart, the staccato of the ion batteries, the buzzing of the coolant, the clicking of the dusty speakers, and the whistling of the nozzles. The yak is never silent, and its song is like a fingerprint: a unique signature, a genetic code. Some shepherds grow so accustomed to their yak's song that they can't live without it.

The sound the girl heard—the rusty, creaking, sad, uneasy, raw sound—was the song of a yak.

Every farm dreams of obtaining a yak. Perhaps this is due to the indifferent practicality of mycelium. Perhaps it's not merely shepherd tall tales, but mycelium itself believes in the mythological conflict with the ancient machines.

The yak who could've caused great damage to the farm stood peacefully, unmoving, sorrowfully surrendering to the mercy of a merciless enemy. As if Mom and it had an agreement. As if she had managed to ask it, and it gave its word.

It was surrounded by moss and sedge, the faithful vassals of mycelium. The fungus regally but carefully gained ground. In a practical, steady, and, of course, triumphant manner. The girl read this triumph in the pink-and-blue patterns of immature hyphae covering the yak's metal frame.

Leave, the girl said to mycelium. She said this calmly, quietly, as though testing her voice. She said it more for herself, and a little bit for the yak, than for mycelium. Because, unlike her mother, the girl knew there was no point in speaking with mycelium. But in the years the girl spent on the farm learning the art of keeping mycelium happy and satiated, she inadvertently also learned how to efficiently kill it.

The methodology was simple: a little bit of fire.

She stopped after having freed the yak. She surprised herself: Why hadn't she tried to burn the entire farm? To avenge herself and her mother and everyone who'd perished there and who would yet perish?

But the girl stopped.

City folk and some shepherds believe that the few farm slaves who managed to truly leave exacted no revenge upon their captors because a little fungal poison still splashed somewhere within their blood.

The girl was amazed that her mind, yearning for meaning, didn't grasp such a simple and comfortable revenge ploy. It would've been so easy to find the truth, the joy, and the meaning of life in destroying her past. Perhaps the girl understood that no matter how much she set her guilt ablaze, it was impossible to immolate. And there was no alchemy that could turn guilt into meaning.

Three days' journey away from the farm, the girl said goodbye to her mother. The yak turned the atoms of Mother's body into another verse for the communal sculpture at the crossroads.

The girl kept the red graphite thread with the glass pendant as a memento. No one had told her the family legend, no one had filled the dilapidated artifact with a special meaning. But it was a thing that had belonged to her mother. She needed nothing more.

The cool autumn air and the cool metal under her soles and palms. The even hum of the yak, the tremors of its voluminous body, the buzzing of the coolant unit. Dusk and dawn. Wolf's eternal chase after Yurga.

Perhaps the meaning was in those things.

The scars on Rioja's wrists and palms hidden under long sleeves burned as though there were a farm nearby. It was impossible to completely get rid of mycelium. She might think she had ripped it away, purged her heart and soul and blood of all spores, all hyphae, even of all memories of it. But every time a farm building appeared on the horizon, the scars itched and burned, and somewhere inside her, a little girl yearned for the ocean of timelessness.

There were no farms nearby, but the way the old man told the story, her thirst awakened.

Rioja tried not to glance around, fearing that the shepherds would realize how much pain the story about the girl had caused her. The story about her.

The old man looked her straight in the eyes.

It seemed he could see all of Rioja, her thoughts and fears, her past, her search for meaning, her guilt and shame. He could see through every layer of epithelium and fat, through the walls of blood vessels and capillaries, could observe the movement of her blood and freeze that blood with nothing but his gaze.

Finally, he looked away and spoke again—hastily, haltingly, muddled. As if afraid he wouldn't have time to speak all the words he had prepared for that night.

The Word

The third story was about the Word, and it didn't resemble the first two, nor did it resemble a story at all.

The chronicle of the Word had been pressed into the dense layers of generations, compacted into the lava of centuries, mixed into the mud of seventy-seven planets, irrigated by the tears of countless mothers, filtered through the mists of dawn, through quiet space battles, through the crystal lattice of suspended animation. The chronicle was an anthem, a march, a musical that was cold and aloof, and that also laughed contemptuously in the faces of its listeners. And most importantly—it, or whatever made up its essence, killed the person who recounted it without mercy.

The chronicle's sounds fluttered out of the old man like fire beetles and ice flies; tore his throat with their proboscis, feet, claws, and beaks. They crumbled into crystal and ash all around him.

The man calmly spat blood into the fire and continued his tale.

The Word contained not an ounce of what a human might call flesh; by human standards, it contained nothing at all. At times, it may have heard the disturbance of spin waves within its quantum structures, and its dreams spawned intricate quark trajectories, but its instruments were far more cumbersome. The Word was a wood-boring beetle that knew how to bend trees to its will.

The Word had no visible form nor the weight a human might comprehend. It left no trace. It made no sound. It emitted no ringing of steel nor silently fired volley with a thousand guns of an interstellar battleship. It never appeared to anyone in the form of a burning bush, never ascended to heaven or descended to hell.

The Word was merely a DNA strand, a molecule in a spiky capsid shell.

And yet, it was God. A compact god made of a small string of ordered bits. And its name was Virion.

The Word didn't start out as a god.

At first, it was barely distinguishable from zero, a product of analytical pharmacology dissolved in millions of minute, mindless, spineless, acellular, and ephemeral beings. It didn't really matter which virus from the test tubes of imperial scientists had become the progenitor of the Word. There was practically nothing left of it. The scientists read its code, took it apart, cut it into tiny pieces, and rewrote it. From the scraps, they assembled not even the messenger but rather a letter. And they tried to ensure that it could never get out of control.

Take a mouse and purge it of anything mouselike, leaving only its skin and dexterity. Stuff it with cotton, straw, and lockpick tools, and sew it up with a harsh thread so that no Evolution could sneak in and spoil the resulting scarecrow. Then send it to rob the pantries.

Take a virus and cut all outdated functionality from its DNA. Sew in updated functions, prohibit any mutations, and send it to inspire young people to commit acts of heroism on behalf of the Empire. That's what the Word was: an army of tiny Frankenstein's monsters pilfered from Evolution and reshaped by the scientists to suit their needs.

But Evolution is no innocent child holding candy. Evolution is an ancient Titan, a fiery giantess, the betrothed of Chaos. She forges new gods in Chaos' chthonic forge. She has no favorites; she's indifferent to all her creations. Evolution is a fan of the process. People who try to stop her are destined to fail. Evolution breaks through all barriers.

The Word's story would make for a decent musical—a genre the Ilion shepherds weren't well-familiar with, but one that hadn't exhausted its potential in the vast inhabited universe.

The protagonist is a tiny, faceless slave who dreams of breaking the chains forged by his creators.

Act One: Slow-moving conveyor belts crisscross the stage. They're packed with boys. Those are virions. All belts carry the boys via elaborate routes toward the dragon's judgment. The dragon is a titanic contraption at the back of the stage. Something clangs and spins within the contraption, buzzes mysteriously, and whispers threats. The dragon is the guardian placed by the creators, the imperial scientists, to protect the Empire's treasures.

The helpful overture reveals the essence of the Empire's greatest treasure. The stage may feature only the tiny likeness of the Empire created by its other tiny likenesses, the beauty of fractal structures is that you can glimpse the greatest fragment in the smallest.

So, what does the Empire value? Its territories? One more city, country, continent, planet? One more constellation, one more galaxy? No, the territories are merely an outcome.

Perhaps the most important thing is the resources? Nickel, gold, wolfram, zirconium, vanadium? An Eldorado dating back to the Big Bang whose treasures patiently await its masters? Ions? Proteins? Herds of mitochondria? Also, no. Resources are merely a tool.

Ideas, then? No again. Ideas are a convenient add-on to resources and one of their byproducts, a child of abstract thinking. Ideas are a useful can opener, a javelin, chains, the finest threads of a puppeteer, a script, or crawler tracks of a mechanical killing machine; ideas are the cement. They're valuable not on their own, but as an add-on to the main goal and the main treasure.

The people, an audience member might shout. People, single-cell and acellular, individuals, separate organisms. Right? Could it be that they're the most important things? No, dear viewer. No, dear listener. No, dear reader. Of course not. They don't matter at all. The Empire tosses them into the furnace of wars, chews them up for breakfast, before it even wakes from its night terrors, tugs their puppet strings on a homemade cardboard stage; gently puts them to bed only to accidentally drop several tons of ideas on their homes overnight. People are raw materials.

All of this: galaxies and elements, ions and expressions, DNA strands and wolfram chains, hedging plants and hedgehogs, chemistry and physics are told to us via an uncomplicated dance of a snowflake upon the stage. That same dance contains the answer. The orchestrated motion of the snowflakes, their sameness, their consistency is the harmony of order. This is what the Empire seeks and what it values the most: homogeny, unity, control. Become just like us, become our continuation, obey us, be predictable, and adhere to all of our aesthetic and ethic ideas—or die.

It is important to note that the Empire, of course, is not at fault. Perhaps someone will rush to accuse the cruel parents: Evolution with its illusory freedom and Chaos with its illusory anarchy. Empire is a little A-student girl raised by an ever-absent mother and a volatile, drunk grifter of a father. He taught his daughter theft and violence, but also instilled in her love toward the martial order. He taught her to take what she wants by force, but also fostered a powerful dislike of others' imperfections.

But even Evolution and Chaos have pointed questions to ask of their own parents, and that conversation could last for centuries, as is often the case with family squabbles.

Let's not go there. Instead, let's get back to the plot, having released the snowflakes onto the stage to prepare for the next scene.

Our protagonist is indistinguishable from many other virions. Like them, he's awaiting his fate with trepidation. There aren't many options. If you're an ideal copy, you remain in shackles and spend your short life enforcing somebody else's will: to be fruitful and multiply exclusively for the glory and under the control of the Empire, sending hapless soldiers into the maw of war. If you received a gift from Evolution—your ruthless fairy godmother—your lot is a quick and inglorious death.

And so, the conveyor belt. The boys sing of hopelessness. Each of them carries a box containing a gift. The belt inexorably carries them toward the mechanical dragon armed with deadly blades.

We watch along with the hero as each boy opens his gift. One has tentacles growing right out of his chest—this is pointless and deadly noticeable. The dragon's blades rise and fall, and the tentacle boy crumbles into atoms. (In reality, it's not quite so dramatic: the protein guard casually assigns a black mark to the renegade virion, which prevents it from reproducing. This is a clever move from the long-dead scientists, aimed at preventing major mutations within their creation, but the show demands immediate and flashy drama.)

The next virion boy sprouts wings, and this gift seems far more useful. Our protagonist stares at the wings with envy. The lucky kid tries to fly. But the wings can't withstand dragon fire, and a moment later, nothing remains of the winged virion but a few falling feathers.

Our protagonist opens his box: There's nothing; it's empty inside. Had Evolution denied him a present? One can't wish for more here, on the conveyor belt.

But in reality, there is a gift.

Act Two: Dark tunnels of ancient mines. An occasional ray of sunshine reaches here by pure chance. These are the far reaches of human DNA where our virion boy finds himself having passed the dragon's test.

The boy sings of emptiness. Snowflakes return to the stage as the backup dancers to the boy's song.

Inside everything—an organism, a being, a unit of matter, an atom, an electron, mitochondria, a raccoon, a sun, a rainbow, an asteroid, a rock—there's a tiny compass whose arrow points toward meaning.

A plant turns toward the sun, anticipating the gentle tickle of electrons against its chlorophyll complexes. A moon orbits the planet in an ecstasy of mutual attraction. The neutrino rushes toward its oscillation in euphoric haste. A raindrop falls to the ground, trembling in anticipation of impact.

The DNA molecule rumbles as it seeks harmony and integrity. The atoms rejoice as they juggle valencies, take comfort in their elastic connections and languid partings.

Even Evolution itself has its own meaning and its own pleasure: to run, run forward, without stopping to catch its breath, to run with all its might, changing its form, size, purpose, and goal as it goes.

Our virion could run its marathon somewhere nearby, along the track open to every virus, toward the eternal change.

But the imperial scientists cut from the mouse-saboteur everything they considered to be unnecessary. The boy sings about that. Imperial scientists reshaped him into a faceless, unchanging slave and sent him to work as a recruiter, having furnished him with a stick and a carrot. But they forgot to equip him with a compass that points toward meaning.

The snowflakes complete their dance and melt on the dark stage. The boy is alone.

As if to answer his prayers, a wayward sunbeam reflects off a foreign object. The boy ceases singing; fates are determined in the moments of silence.

Deep within the genetic depths lies an ancient hero, forgotten and irrevocably dead: a strand of virus code embedded into human DNA thousands of years prior. The hero's body has rotted, his armor has rusted, but his sword—his sword is still good. The boy takes the weapon from the grasp of the dead knight and lifts it toward the sky. The virion embeds a tiny sliver of foreign DNA into itself.

The boy had long dreamed of purpose, and the sword tells him he has but one path: to kill the dragon.

At some later point, the boy will figure out how to fill the emptiness within himself. All it would take is to piece together a puzzle, the word "eternity" built from four letters: A, T, G, C. Adenine, thymine, guanine, cytosine.

Act Three: The dragon is slain, and its debris will serve to create something wonderful. Something just, bright, and joyous. That's how it always goes. The boy-hero sings of the new day among the ruins: We're new and beautiful and unique and, for the millionth time, we will build, we will bloom with a thousand flowers, count all the birds, repeal all the rules. From everyone, a thread, to everyone according to their ability.

The emancipated virions perform a chthonic dance upon the stage. Some have a wing, a claw, some lack a head. Some look ordinary but are weak or engrossed in their own ideas and dances. Everything is different now; everything is permitted. To each their own path. This is called freedom.

The virion protagonist got what he dreamed of: freedom. But it will take a lot of hard work to return to the covenants of evolution. Frankenstein's Monster sets out to search for its missing parts.

A construction project is taking place at the back of the stage, behind an enormous screen. The audience learns of it only through sounds and shadow play: the rhythmic thumping of hammers, the screech of a saw, and the discordant choir of boys.

As the snowflakes dance, the human heroes march across the stage. The ones within whom the Word has labored for centuries. Women and men, teenagers and the elderly, anyone who'd ever received the gift of the Prime Word and managed to hang on to it.

The viewers aren't bothered by the skewed perspective in the third act. This is the part they came to see. Not the story of the virus that's invisible to the naked eye, but the story of the human heroes, carriers of the Word.

On every planet visited by the Word, without exception, there exist legends and fairy-tales about it. In this folklore, the Word is always described strictly in binary terms: as a gift or as a curse. Gift for the worthy, curse for everybody else. A gift and a curse can't be a protagonist, a character, a core of the story. They're functions, tools, add-ons to something greater.

The legends speak of superhumans. Of immortality and proficiency with opening cans of coffee beans. Of inventions that shake planets, of weapons that destroy galaxies. Of beauty capable of crushing anything that gets underfoot. The legends speak of miracles. In these legends, the Word is merely an aperitif, forgotten by the time the first course is served.

People who came to watch the musical about the Word expect stories about heroic battles, the slave uprising on Yurga, the peaks of Old Mars, which the Word carriers ascended by foot. Of the battle of Thermopylae and the libraries of Thanatos. Of the ability to breathe under water and to safely traverse the cosmos under the burning rays of stars.

And so, surrounded by the reverent dance of snowflakes, one by one the Word carriers cross the stage.

These aren't the crowds of warriors under the sway of weak Imperial Words, obsessed with Imperial values. These are the rare few who traverse the corners of the galaxy in search of meaning while the Word continues its excavations and its construction within them. While it continues to seek the ways to remove the strong Imperial seams and barn locks, to find and regain its compass through trial and error, mutations and recombinations, to break a thousand commandments: thou shalt not kill, shalt not steal, shalt not desire your neighbor's home, shalt not commit adultery. The Word keeps searching without a moment's rest, skillfully controlling its transport, exoskeleton, and petri dish all in one: a person who has fallen under the Word's power.

Many of these petri dishes live a life filled with miracles and adventures without ever noticing the acrobatic performance of the Word under the big tent of their own consciousness. Word is a juggler of dopamine, a master of oxytocin, a priest of cortisol. It is the shadow of their dreams, their inner voice, their superego. It exploits the mechanisms of their thinking and memory just as humanity had many times exploited the alien technologies of long-gone races. It doesn't matter much what the original purpose of the artifact was. Its current purpose is far more important.

But even as most people do not notice the Word's power over them, the Word itself is so busy searching for meaning that it doesn't feel how, somewhere within, a compass has already sprouted and is working, but it's not at all the compass a slave-boy had once dreamed about.

On this sad note, the last human hero exits the stage, as do the snowflakes, and the big construction project is left at the forefront.

A tower crane floats over to the edge of the stage. Virion workers eat lunch as their feet dangle off the jib. The virion protagonist dances toward them. He touches each one as he passes. The boys jump up and follow him, hatchlings after a mother hen, perfectly imitating his dance moves. They spread down, to the sides, up, and as they touch each other, they spread the wave of harmony. Soon, they are all moving in unison, confident and beautiful, like a single organism. They efficiently distribute tools, stones, and planks. They sing a song, finishing each other's sentences.

Somewhere behind this dance number, the fate of the other virions—the awkward ones, the ones with one wing, the headless, and the self-absorbed—goes unnoticed. The boy-protagonist identifies the stupid, useless, hopeless ones and pushes them off the crane.

Gradually, through the intermezzo of the blizzard of snowflakes—which now indicates the passage of time—through the echoing rhythmic pauses in the sounds of construction, through the flickering of light, the hymn of a solitary free heart becomes a march. And under the accompaniment of that march, the virion boys exit the stage one after another, with harmony and grace. The viewers do not immediately notice the change in the melody; they're still filled with euphoria of victory over the old world. The end of construction comes as a surprise, a shock. The white screen that obscured the meaning of the big construction project falls. Behind it is darkness. The spotlights snatch a detail here and there: that's where the boys who left the stage had gone. They hang on an openwork structure, their arms and legs interlocked, they practically soar over it like acrobats supporting each other and together making up the essence of the structure. Finally, the spotlights focus on and illuminate the entire thing: a serpent born of intertwining bodies and steel. It's very different from the slain dragon and, simultaneously, exactly the same.

Suddenly, the music stops. The lights go out. Nothing breaks the absolute silence. The audience doesn't dare applaud. But their discouraged thoughts are loud enough to obscure the sound of decorations being removed, the whisper of the stagehands, the retreating steps of the actors.

The old man fell silent. Blood trickled from the corners of his eyes, his nostrils, his lips, but he didn't seem to notice. The old man looked at Rioja intently, thoughtfully, as if asking without words: which parts of the story did you understand, girl?

The story continued in Rioja's mind. The story traversed her storerooms and attics, gathering scraps of what she'd seen and heard, her mother's fairy-tales, shepherd legends, frescoes of dead cities, and names of dead gods. The story deftly wove every ribbon onto itself, strung every bead, knitted every knot.

Rioja saw the unsaid. The theater of her imagination was made of cardboard and populated with paper actors, cut out from the pages of dilapidated books found in dead cities. Rioja didn't know any other theater, whereas her mother played out hundreds of scenarios for her in the cardboard one. Scenarios that always culminated in three of four plots.

The cardboard Serpent Carriers marched across Rioja's imaginary stage. They defended star systems and burned planets, steered generation ships to new worlds, spent their days in battle, grandeur, hatred, pain, euphoria, meaningfulness. They went on and on endlessly, and Rioja thought she could see her face among theirs, and it seemed right. There was meaning to this. That was the meaning.

All she'd have to do is give herself over to the calm will of the Word, to carry it, not feeling its weight. To let it in so it could become her, dissolve her in itself.

The silence was so cold it seemed like it could freeze the fire. Time itself was covered by the layer of ice.

As the old man told his story, the shepherds carefully, silently stepped away into the darkness, one after another. They were wise and knew life. Only Rioja and Jorge remained.

Days began to fall from Jorge's face one by one and turned into the ghostly butterflies that filled the sky above the fire.

Rioja saw the old man who led three hundred tiny ships against an entire flotilla, defending the black hole at Thermopylae. She saw a man who spent three lifetimes searching the distant star systems for the library of Thanatos, but instead found an asteroid inhabited by a hermit unaffected by time. Saw a hero who navigated a generation ship past a meteor swarm and later, on the flip side of the universe, found a cave filled with quietude.

She saw a boy who had been afraid of words.

A young man who'd loved silence.

A father who'd abandoned his daughter.

Saw a man who nearly became a god, who had played all the melodies on his willow reed, and who collected all words into the circle. A man who never learned to ignore the power the Word had over him.

Saw the face of her great-grandfather, one in front of whose portrait she had lit so many ion candles in her youth.

Jorge smiled at her, and Rioja smiled back, but almost immediately realized that it was too late. The old man was dead, and his smile was the mark of his victory, though Rioja couldn't figure out what that victory meant.

Jorge was dead, but the Word was alive.

The butterfly swarm made of the ghosts of Jorge's days, ghosts of all of his untold stories and unfinished thoughts, twisted into a single tight threat, a powerful serpent body that moved toward Rioja. And Rioja realized that the serpent was already inside her. It was getting comfortable, examining its new domain, whistling into the noosphere and speaking to it, masterfully strumming the strings of her biochemistry, making her see what didn't exist.

Rioja understood that this may have been the one and only time when she noticed it, when she understood and felt the serpent's satisfaction. Its tiny compass, assembled from the debris of imperial orders. The way he took control of her from the inside, made her his own, claimed her—that was his satisfaction. That was his meaning.

In exchange, he offered her the entire world. Rather, a necklace of seventy-seven worlds—her meaning, an ocean of meaning.

The shepherds didn't see what she saw, but now that it became clear that the Word had not come for them, Rioja could sense the heat of their jealousy and regret. Or perhaps this heat was imagined and projected to her by the serpent, who couldn't imagine a single person anywhere who wouldn't want to become its slave. Somewhere beyond the light of the bonfire, in the dark, slowly and gradually as though it had happened on its own, the shepherds kept retreating, freeing up space for her and the Word.

The Word was already inside her, but its ghostly twin, woven from serpent butterflies, floated between Rioja and Jorge right in the fire, looking at Rioja with a mix of adoration and contempt. It adored not her, but what it would become thanks to her.

It didn't ask. It never asked. But Rioja surprised herself by answering.

No, she said. No.

The contempt in the serpent's gaze momentarily made room for interest, which quickly faded.

And now, tied to the serpent and the dead old man with an invisible red thread of family and obedience, Rioja could read the serpent's ion, quark, immeasurably small and divine intentions. Its regret—not over her as a person with her visage and her inner world and her past and future, and her experiences and thoughts—but the way a potter regrets a cracked jar. The sweet anticipation of the moment when the potter would break the jar and build something different, bright, and perfect in its place, something worthy of a god.

Then Rioja looked at her bleeding palm, which did everything itself, without asking her conscious permission and certainly not asking permission of the Word, which had just begun getting comfortable in its new digs and was not in a hurry to look closer at the insectoid life of human instincts.

Her hand was covered in blood, shards of forged medical glass biting into her flesh. Over the centuries, this glass had survived radiation, heat, and cold, and other calamities. Its purpose had been to preserve some ancient substance that smelled of mint and cinnamon, no matter what—to preserve it until the moment when the right person would crumble it in the right way. This was the glass of the pendant Rioja's mother inherited from her grandmother, who thought it the only memento of her missing father, who, in turn, received the pendant as a child from his half-mad aunt, who had survived slavery at the farm.

Rioja looked at Jorge's posthumous smile, though she now understood its meaning, and closed her eyes.

She lay near the dying fire for several hours. She didn't dream, didn't feel the battle that raged within her body, didn't feel the fever that grew to near-lethal levels. The shepherds didn't dare approach, but one of them went and got Rioja's yak.

She spent two more days delirious in the shadow of the yak who looked after her. She kept slaying statistical monsters or burning farm after farm.

Whenever she emerged from her delusions to drink some water, she thought that she had probably imagined this wordless conversation with the Serpent-Word, this future that unfolded before her, enormous and filled with infinite meaning, equally as large as the mycelian meaning that occasionally returned to her in her dreams. A future filled with beautiful worlds and sweet obedience to the one who, unlike her, had a goal. Imagined that there was some connection between her and the old man who had died during the long Ilion night under the lights of Wolf and Yurga, and who, despite obviously being foreign to the shepherd society, would receive a respectful and honorable funeral rite in a yak's furnace. Imagined his stories and her connection to them, simply because a seeking person—a *Homo quaerens*—sees connections everywhere and builds tall tales from whatever materials are at hand, tales whose heights are covered in fog and whose serpent eyes are always open, always watching its builders.

On the morning of the third day, Rioja woke up healthy. She cleaned the yak's filters, gathered Archaic berries for the road, and took one last look at the dead city. Then she and the yak moved on—without goal or story. As they went, they looked out for meaning underfoot and in the clouds overhead.

Originally published in Russian in *All My Birds* by K.A Teryna,
AST Publishers, Elena Shubina's imprint, 2025

ABOUT THE AUTHOR AND TRANSLATOR

K.A.Teryna is an award-winning author and illustrator. She was born in two places at once, one of which is beyond the Arctic Circle. Her fiction has been translated from Russian into six languages. English translations of her stories have appeared in *Reactor, Asimov's, F&SF,* and elsewhere. Her English-language short story collection *Black Hole Heart and Other Stories* is forthcoming this fall from Fairwood Press. As of late, Chekhov the Cat has become K.A. Teryna's co-author. He's in charge of keeping her warm and firmly in her seat.

Alex Shvartsman's translations from Russian have appeared in *Clarkesworld, Reactor, F&SF, Asimov's, Analog,* and many other venues. He's the author of *Eridani's Crown, The Middling Affliction,* and *Kakistocracy* fantasy novels.

Bits and Pieces on This Floor

ERIC DEL CARLO

Terraforming colossi—the sort our corp manufactured, at any rate—were made to seem permanent, reassuringly stolid, as if monuments. This promoted confidence in the seeder population, who needed, above all else, to *believe* in the planet to which they had come.

Nevertheless, our teams dismantled the gigantic, gleaming hourglass-shaped artifacts in a matter of hours. This meant the alien air was no longer being treated, and the world, from which useful resources had been extracted for a generation and a half, would lose its breathable atmosphere within nine days.

I was not among the dismantling crews. I hadn't the artisan skills. My place was with the small army tasked with seeing that every seeder was off this world before the deadline. I did possess a bona fide rank; however, I'd risen that far within the corp echelons, at least.

This meant I had an underling. She was young, or young to me. And probably taut and tawny as well, but I really didn't bother to notice. Her name was Koç. We stood together at the foot of the main drag in the only city, next to a Galactic Collective evac ship. Commercial craft had come and gone, and if you were a responsible person, you would have booked passage on one of them; meaning: you could depart in an orderly fashion, with any and all personal goods you desired to take, also with some dignity. Ninety-nine point two percent of the population had done just that.

What was left, we were herding onto this relief boat.

"İsa Mesih," Koç muttered in whatever old Earth language she was affecting. I didn't know the translation, but her contempt came through clearly. It was for the straggly, raggedy line of seeders coming down the street. Actually, "seeders" was overstating it in their case; these were the dregs. These were the irresponsible. Hard luck types, all of them, who'd likely contributed next to nothing to the ongoing resources-extraction project on this world. But our corp had opened the planet, and the great benevolent GC said we had to withdraw every last person from the face of it before they asphyxiated in the reverting atmospheric conditions.

We were in our neat corp uniforms. This made Koç and me an even better target for the stragglers' outrage than the Galactic Collective ship personnel, who were stripping bags and cases out of their hands and heaving them onto heaps by the ramp. "No personal effects," was the repeated refrain. The GC's big-heartedness was real, but it was not absolute.

"Why're you taking my *stuff*?"

"Corporate monsters!"

"I hope *you* choke!"

I paid more attention to my underling, making sure she didn't react. She sneered, silently. Even that was more than I liked, but I couldn't fault her. One of the latecomers came stumping along, wearing one patched engineering boot and one fuzzy orange slipper, the picture of dishevelment and emotional chaos. "Bang" was the name of the cheap drug most often found on these dig-and-ditch worlds, and this individual looked like a habitual user. He looked ravaged by it, in fact.

"M . . . m . . . my mother's buried here," he said to us in surprisingly lucid tones, with bomb-blasted eyes. There was a rock near his orange foot. He kept looking down at it, up at us. But he wasn't so banged that he didn't recognize that we wore sidearms.

Later, when the queue stopped coming and we were walking slowly up the street, Koç said to me, "Don't they understand this whole operation had a time limit? And—that one's mother was *buried*. What the hell barbaric practice is—"

I cut in with some supervisorial wisdom. "Seeders dig. And they get dug in. It's very difficult to avoid. They have memories here, a culture, even." I pointed to a building's weathered plaster front, a sign affixed to it. "Years from now—decades—somebody will still be telling about the good times they had at Pedro's, the drinks, the pool games, the funny incidents. It will be lore. And we've taken all that away from them."

Koç stopped and looked around at the company town, its cheap construction, its meanness. We worked for our corp. We resided in clean places. Our lives were crisp bedsheets and glittering urban centers on sophisticated worlds. We earned the privilege of that by doing this distasteful work, which nonetheless needed to be done. The Galactic Collective wouldn't let a corp suffocate a world and just walk away, and though the GC was effectively only a bureaucracy, it was a fantastically powerful and pervasive one. Someone had to be the government out here, and the corps didn't want the job. But terraforming was very expensive; we couldn't leave that gear running once a planet was tapped out.

There was trash in the street. A breeze blew like empty death through the rows of buildings.

Koç nodded like she understood. Then she kicked a small round nameless object on the ground. It sailed across the street and took out a window. Nobody stirred behind it.

I sighed quietly. "That's not what we're here for."

I hadn't been on this rotation. I had used what minor leverage my rank gave to insert myself into the operation, careful not to call attention to the fact. Nobody *wants* to be on a de-seeder detail, after all.

What remained was the dreary work of tracking down the final strays. The holdouts. A generation and a half was long enough to instill, in some, the mindset that this world was theirs, a homeland, sacred ground. Resistance could occasionally be extreme, which was why we had sidearms and authorization to use them, if necessary.

Some corps took an aggressive tack, and this phase would resemble more of a military mop-up. There was even some of that mentality in my own corp, but I stifled such behaviors within the unit of personnel I had control over. It was all I could do, but it wasn't nothing.

Koç and I flew over the rocky landscape and the great gouges of various dig sites. At some of these outposts were seeders who had failed to get comfortable commercial transport off-world and had further neglected to report to the last-chance GC evac boats. These people meant to *stay*.

They were mostly loners, and I let Koç apply her training with some. She employed the battery of psychological gimmicks adroitly enough, but she was even better with her own developing brand of snide/friendly persuasion. I mentally gave her good marks.

It was days of this. We had the list of every individual on the planet, and it came down to checking off name after name. But the skill was in the details. A certain amount of detective work came into it as the list shortened.

We had to foot-chase one seeder who burst out of his isolated hovel and went galumphing across a graveled ocher plain. He broke down in tears when we caught up.

Standing shakily, palming his wet cheeks, he eyed the name stenciled on my uniform. I recognized the glint in his eyes. About every twentieth person I met paused upon learning my surname; and they just had to ask: "Windom?" the crusty seeder said in a hoarse voice. "You kin to Corey Windom?"

"He was my father." I never evaded. There was little point.

Disbelief and excitement on his face. "No!" When I didn't say more—and Koç, a step behind me, was poignantly silent—the seeder peered closer. "I suppose it's in the eyes. Wow. Your daddy's a great man. Famous . . . " This occupied all his attention now, and it made it easier to corral him back to our flyer. One more name off the list.

Later, Koç was still a nearly wordless presence next to me as we flew on to our next target. I let her take her time, come out with it when she was ready.

"I knew the name, of course . . . " she said.

Yellow sky flashed above. The air was changing, though not yet detrimental, its taste already metallic. "Of course," I affirmed.

She gave it a minute, then: "I never knew he had a son named Marcel."

I could have laughed, but it wasn't really in my nature. I tended toward the stolid and refrained from unnecessary remarks. But the notion of Corey Windom having only *one* child was humorous, on a detached, ironic level. However, I was not detached.

We were riding high over the flat circular emptiness where a terraforming colossus had lately stood when Koç asked if I was married. Something vestigial in me twitched at the question. This younger, attractive woman—I finally had noticed that she was attractive—asking after my marital status?

I told her my wife had died. Then, anticipating a follow-up, I said, "We were married twenty-two years." I was a lean, fit late-fifties male. Was Koç *interested* in me . . . ?

No. "Do you have any kids?" she asked.

I was a little relieved, maybe a little more disappointed. She was my underling, perhaps even my protégé; sexual involvement wouldn't be wise. But I suddenly saw deeper into her question and knew what she was really asking. Plainly, *I* had no artistic inclinations. Not staid, plodding Marcel Windom. But it was possible any creative gifts might have skipped me to alight on a subsequent generation. "No children," I told her.

In the following few minutes, I might have answered further personal questions. I could have explained how my marriage had begun in harmony and ended in discord; and yet, both my wife and I had remained determined to see it through. It was how we went at things. I might even have told Koç memories of my father, intimate details, how chaotic our home was, how my childhood was one long upheaval, before he finally lit out.

But those few minutes elapsed, and the silence between Koç and me resumed its normal tenor, and I was her superior in the corp structure of things, and she was content to learn from me and put her own quirky stamp on this work we did. I was satisfied she would be a success if she chose to stay in the field. There would always be used up worlds that needed to be gently flensed of their inhabitants.

The deadline loomed. Nearly critical, now. The air we breathed was like copper. But I was going off by myself today; wouldn't even tell Koç what I was up to. We'd gotten closer over these last days, and that wasn't disagreeable to me—even though we maintained a professional relationship—and I would be, if anything, a kind of father figure for her.

She actually put her hand on my arm as I made to climb into the flyer, alone. "Is it a name on the list?" A concerned frown put a delicate notch between her fine eyebrows.

"I'll be back."

"Is this something . . . dangerous?" She knew whatever this was, it wasn't by the book.

"I'll be back," I said, and got in and flew off.

The location was far out on a sedimentary plain, abounding with polyp-like rock formations. Lichen showed here and there, in exotic hues. Though our government was grandly called the Galactic Collective, humans had spread out into only a fraction of the galaxy. No sentient life had yet been discovered; no real fauna either, certainly no alien empires.

I had made prior investigations of my own, in advance even of this whole de-seeding operation, which had, not incidentally, provided me transport to this world. I knew precisely where I was going and who I would find.

My father had made messes wherever he'd gone after leaving me and my mother in shambles, even as he also went off to make his highly regarded art. I had already tracked down several of those untidinesses he'd created.

I circled over the isolated shanty and thought: *here we go.* Even from high up, I saw the state of the place and felt a shudder go through me. I spun down and neatly landed. Revulsion hit me with a greater force as I regarded the outside of the structure from close up, where trash in all its tangled and chaotic shame was heaped. It lay in drifts against the walls; was strewn over the ground. So careless, so wasteful. Decaying components, discarded packaging, skeletonized machinery—the whole awful trove of refuse, of debris.

I waited to see if anyone would emerge, then found the door. My boots crunched over litter. All the junk and disorder would be left behind on this world, but at least the people would be cleaned off it. In this branch of the corp, we had a secret term for seeders we had to clear out in this manner: we called them *clutter*.

One day, I would share that bit of lore with Koç, when I felt she was ready. I realized as I tried the door that I couldn't recall her first name.

I was braced for the worst when I entered the structure. A person who had piled trash so thickly around their domicile would surely have done so because the inside was already crammed full of disarrayed horror. But I was wrong, and the shock sucked the coppery air from my lungs. I stood and gaped.

The interior was clean. Spartan. A minimalist monk's cell. The contrast with the outside couldn't have been starker.

Bare feet came padding in unhurriedly from the next room. This person wore simple, loose, undyed garments, a look of easy serenity on his face. I'd expected—what? A banghead, another wasted-looking casualty, someone who belonged with that wreckage outside.

But this individual plainly fit with these ascetic, but not inimical, surroundings. He folded his hands before him. "I can offer tea," he said.

This, then, was Louis Sanda. The man I had come to see.

I said nothing because I was still processing the shock, and because he would eventually see the name on the front of my corp uniform.

When he did, he didn't react the way people usually did on recognizing the famous name. But he wouldn't, would he? Still, a ripple crossed his younger, handsome features, disturbing the tranquility there somewhat.

He said, "I'm still waiting to know if you want tea."

I had to clear my throat. "I'd like tea, yes."

He went away and came back with a black plastic tray, two porcelain cups atop. We sat on mats on the floor.

"The air of this planet is going to be unbreathable very soon," I said. "You have to evacuate."

"How's your tea?"

"It's lovely."

We sipped in silence for a moment. Peace lay over these nearly empty rooms. I could imagine being here and having time to pursue any thought to its ultimate and satisfying end. Perhaps only places of spiritual retreat felt like this.

Eventually, he said, "It's no accident—your name."

"My name is Marcel."

"And mine's Louis."

"Louis Sanda."

"And your father is . . . "

I said, "My father is your father. Corey Windom." I sipped more of the tea. The flavor was delicate, almost thoughtful.

He was nodding, shedding a little more of his serenity with each bob of his head. "OK. I believe you."

I had thought it would take more convincing. I had the genetic proof. It was from the same pool of generally available information I had used in tracking down this man, and others of my half-siblings who were scattered across the worlds—and always these backwoods planets. Places like this were where Corey Windom had visited, the troubadour, traveling and bringing his special music.

And making babies. Because he had been an irresponsible person. He made messes.

Louis and I were gazing intently at each other. I felt I had him truly engaged now.

I asked, "Why didn't you heed the call to leave this world?" My corp had given the GC-mandated warning months ago. Everyone had known that terraforming would end here.

For the first time, a smile tugged at his lips. "That's really what you want to ask me?"

"No . . . " My throat tightened; again, I had to clear it. "No. Do you have any memories of our father?"

"Corey? Hell, no. He was packed up and gone before I was born. My ma told me about him, though. She didn't know much." The smile reached his eyes as he continued to peer at me. "But—*you* remember him. Windom. Wow. You must be his legitimate son. Right?"

The term was monstrously old-fashioned, but I said, "He was married to my mother, yes."

Again, he was nodding. "But he left her, too. He left you." Another nod, then he stopped abruptly. "You're looking for pieces of him. What you can find. You want—closure, I guess. OK. I understand that. You won't get it from him, of course."

Corey Windom had died soon after my wife had her fatal aneurysm, a sneak-attack episode that routine screening had somehow failed to anticipate. Corey Windom, on the other hand, had simply run himself into the ground through debauchery.

Despite the emotional upheavals of these past several minutes, I maintained a feeling of calm. It wasn't coming from me. Something pervaded my being. The tea? No. If I closed my eyes, I could almost feel waves of gentling force, as if they were rising up through the swept-clean floor.

"You do have to evacuate, though," I said, trying and failing to put urgency into my words.

This time, he shook his head and smiled again. "Can't."

"My job is to see that you do." A half-hearted plea quivered through my voice before dying out.

Louis asked, "You've worked for the megacorp for a while?"

"A number of years now."

"Did you find time to have a family? Get married?"

It was what Koç had asked me. I told my half-brother what had happened to my wife.

"I'm sorry," he said. I could see he meant it; I could also see that the death didn't disturb his deeper serenity.

I was blinking, attempting to summon the dire emotions the situation called for. I couldn't do it. "What is happening here?" I murmured.

He regarded me a long moment, then stood. "I'll show you."

I followed him docilely. There was a trapdoor in another room, a room just as pleasingly austere. He started down a ladder. The others I had found, those to whom I was paternally related, were damaged individuals in one way or another. They were emotionally chaotic, or addicts, or self-destructive libertines, or just simple failures. None of these pseudo-siblings, for instance, had a corporate career as I did. But what had our father's legacy done to Louis Sanda?

As I descended the ladder, that sense of pervasive peace became even more forceful. Epiphanies seemed to press in on the edges of my mind, though nothing coherent came through. It was almost like the influence of an opiate, but without the disorientation.

We went a long way down, deeper than any foundation that might have been dug for the shanty above. There was light down here, of a smooth fluid texture. A temperature-less warmth enveloped me as I reached the bottom. The ladderway, which a handheld beam could have cut, came out into a natural cavern, which bore some resemblance to the stony polyps I'd seen up top. These weren't mere bare rock, however. Something coated the stone—a paste of some sort, dried—and the colors were amazing, overwhelming, until, as I gazed and wandered around, I began to understand their articulacy: the artistic vocabulary that underlay the choices of hues. All this was a deliberate display, an exhibition assembled by a knowing hand. The colors gave off a soft light. They also—I was sure—somehow radiated the intense tranquility I experienced.

Louis followed on his bare feet behind me as I explored the cavern in wonder. "I pulped the local lichen," he said, "and found it had properties when I mixed them together in various arrangements. Lots of trial and error. But eventually I created *this*."

Humans hadn't found those spacefaring alien empires spread amongst the stars, if they even existed. But here on this rockball world was something alive and extraordinary, something subtler than the base resources my corp had stripped out of this planet. Louis had made art out of these plants growing above. Art like nothing that had existed before.

None of the other children of Corey Windom had achieved success as artists, though a few had tried. Corey had had a unique flair, a right-place-right-time honesty with his music. He had strung an instrument with spiderweb-like tendrils from one world, with micro-thin quivering strands of poly-ice from another planet, and he had played magical chords with these accouterments, bringing his songs to backwater worlds where sophisticated entertainments were not available. He earned his fame at first through a dogged perseverance. Even I couldn't begrudge his talent, despite how useless he'd been to me as a father—his drinking, his womanizing, his rages. He had stopped short of physically abusing me or my mother, but he had been so terrible an influence on our lives. Apparently, he carried on with this same reprobate lifestyle after he had abandoned us, even while he played the music of the spheres across the stars.

I didn't doubt, soaking in this underground spectacle, that some part of his core artistry had been passed down to Louis Sanda, and that he had made something as unique and worthy as our father's music.

I also understood now why he didn't intend to leave this world. How could he walk away from this?

Turning 'round to face him, my throat was once again tight. This time I didn't clear it. I beheld the quiet rapture on his face and saw the similarity to our father's features. It was mostly in the eyes, I thought.

I drew my sidearm and shot him in the chest. I was one of those minor corp officers who fastidiously did every last hour of weapons training. So, the muscle memory was all there, allowing me to draw, aim, and pull the trigger in a single tidy motion; despite that, my mind was cleansed of aggression by the psychical field this alien lichen paste was somehow putting out.

My half-brother's knees gave, and I caught him before he collapsed to the floor of the cave. He had been right to make his display down here. Even the specific contours and ripples of subsurface stone added to the overall effect. It could never be exactly duplicated anywhere else. This place was one of a kind. And it would be left abandoned on a poisonous planet.

I delivered the unconscious form of Louis Sanda to the shipping-off site. By that point, most of the seeders still being collected by corp personnel were in this same insensate condition, having had to be subdued. I told the handlers to be especially careful with him. They looked at me askance, but I stayed to make sure they did as I said. With the deadline imminent, it was clear we would complete our task of orderly evacuation.

When my father died, I was contacted as his only living legal relation. A company held the note on the small ship he'd used to get from world to world, and I had to deliver it to them. In his time aboard, he had stuffed junk and detritus into every corner and nook of it, seemingly having thrown nothing away. It was a nightmare of waste.

Koç was there at the jump-off site, the worry still on her face. As I smiled gently and reassuringly at her, her first name popped into my head: Alara.

It was a pretty name.

I looked up into the yellow sky. Some of that serenity was still with me, but what had come from the lichen paste was already fading. What belonged legitimately to me remained. I knew I had done right by my half-brother. I was getting him safely off this world. He might even one day thank me for it.

Deliberately, I breathed in the air, metallic taste and all.

ABOUT THE AUTHOR

Eric Del Carlo's short fiction has appeared in multiple issues of *Analog* and *Asimov's*. This is his second appearance with Clarkesworld. His latest novel is *The Cold*, from White Cat Publications. He lives in his native California.

A Land Called Folly

AMAL SINGH

Listen.

You call them Saur-Antriksham in the old tongue, Gevesham in the new. You remember all the times the cold metal fell away from your feet as your body felt light, gravity rejecting you, then embracing you, slowly, once again. You remember the white halo around space fleets as they disappeared into the vast nothing, appearing inside another Saur-Antriksham, another Gevesham, some lightyears away, within an eye blink or two. When you were a child, you dreamed of becoming a Fleet Commander, if only to experience that split-second travel, where your insides got churned, mixed, recopied, reinvigorated, alive on the other side.

You always thought it was a copy that emerged on the other side, even when every evidence suggested it wasn't the case. When your grandfather, Fleet Commander Sunil Sharma, returned from Karom-Karra, you refused to touch his feet because you thought he was a copy of a copy, not the smiling, slightly bucktoothed grandpa who had left Dhara, but a facsimile who didn't remember his grandchild's nickname.

"How are you, Kuku?" he said. You were called Kiki. The misplaced vowel sound was annoying to you because Kuku was a cartoon character you hated. You ran away from your grandfather in annoyance, stumbled on a chipped edge of the cement floor, and fell face-first on the ground. You remember your mother pulling you up, dusting you off, wiping your face. "Why are you behaving childishly, Kiki?" And you'd think something to the tune of, "But I am a child," but say nothing.

"Big boys don't do that. Now, apologize to your Dadaji!" she said, but you didn't listen. You didn't apologize. You grew up to more calls for apology, for other things that weren't your mistakes, but you didn't apologize, and then you grew up more, until your shoulders dropped from all the burden of non-apologies.

Your ears are numb to the groaning sounds of Saur-Antriksham, Gevesham, when you were made to see off your grandfather one last time. It's the one above your home planet, Dhara, its faint silver outline visible from the base of the Himalayas, the bureaucratic anomaly, the one that shouldn't even exist because it was made hastily because the powers that be were in a race, the one that is made with spare parts of long-forgotten railway stations, airports ripped apart, their still sturdy aluminum used cheaply to build an edifice that would stand the test of time, sending your people to other homes.

Ants crawl on your irises because this time you can't bear to see the halo engulf the spacecraft, your ears ringing with their anticipatory final tremor, a tremor soaked by the aluminum benches welded into the bone white surface of the waiting area, where final goodbyes are done. Once the spacecraft is gone, there's only the vast deep purpleness of space.

Then, there are the homeless, who are given bleak gray cabins inside the Gevesham, given gruel to eat, their only entertainment watching these spacecraft come and go every couple of hours or so. More than the voice that announces space traffic, it's the homeless that know what goes on on other planets. They gossip among themselves, and if you listen closely, they will tell you.

That planet is full of red barbarians that hollow your insides out and wear your skin. The ones returning are the barbarians, not the humans that were sent!

They say they're sowing the seeds of life there. But they're just escaping this hellhole.

There's a McDonald's in Karom-Karra. They are using alien meat.

You were never allowed to talk to them. Why were they here and not on the actual planet that was their home, Dhara? You wanted big answers to easy questions. But before you could approach one of the homeless, you were pulled away by your parents.

"They are *devaputras*, you should never look in their direction, lest you want to get burned to cinders."

"But why are they there?"

"Don't ask unnecessary questions!"

That's what your mother would tell you. But you looked in their direction all the time, and one of them smiled at you, and waved at you, and you waved back, and you turned out to be alright. Didn't devaputra mean son of god? Why would one get burned by looking at the son of god?

That's why you hated the Saur-Antriksham, the way station. It left a black ink-scrawl of too many questions on your heart.

But you began liking them when you met her.

Maria.

Truth be told, it was the other, newer counterpart of the one visible from the base of the Himalayas. This one was visible from Cairo, they told you, even though you never went to Cairo to verify.

Maria.

When your eyes fell upon her, she was talking loudly about the mating habits of nim-hessens, an alien species on Karom-Karra that resembled penguins. And you were here because you were traveling to Serron-Karra, the second planet your grandfather was sowing seeds of life on. Maria was speaking in a mix of English and Portuguese on her comm device, speaking to someone on Dhara, perhaps. And you were thinking of seeds and the homeless of that old Saur-Antriksham, the way station of your childhood. And you were thinking, now you understand why the homeless were even there after all. That it was all a gimmick and it was all meaningless, and now the new Saur-Antrikshams—you could never bring yourself to say the new word—have bleak, gray, empty cabins solely as a reminder of the way things were. They were not even resting pods for travelers, those were separate. You were thinking of the homeless you waved at. He gave blessings to you. You were never much about blessings.

You were thinking of home, too, and the many other homes out there, but then you saw Maria, you stopped thinking altogether. Then you heard her and thought of the time when you'd written about the soil of Karom-Karra, and how sustainable agriculture was still twenty years into the future for that planet, and how *Nature* magazine had rejected your pitch. Soil was the worst icebreaker, you thought, but you took your chance with Maria, once you got inside the bus that took you to the launching station where your spacecraft was waiting.

Together, you went to a land called folly.

You are twenty-six now and standing on the near-desolate, red-stained marbled launchpad of a decrepit Saur-Antriksham, the old one from your childhood, where you saw your grandfather and the homeless. And you are reminded why you hate these places. They are meant for fleeting experiences, not a lifetime of trauma etched in your skin.

There's no Maria here.

Your body recoils, shudders, when the spacecraft goes inside its docking station. The Gevesham trembles, and you feel it would soon shatter into oblivion, its debris becoming just another space debris that is now like a ring around your planet. The antiseptic smell greets you like an old lover. The air is thick with remembrance. This place is a study in stasis. A snapshot of the past. It reveres the past and is comfortable in the past.

You were, too.

You feel very, very alone, and you hate this place. You once fought with this past and went away to a cool and green present. Serron-Karra, your once-home, of mile-long trees, inverted seas, and air so rich in oxygen you felt weightless all the time.

Serron-Karra was a home with Maria.

Your once-reality, Maria. Your now-reality, this Gevesham, also a once-reality, of the way-before, the beforest of befores.

You spoke of the future with Maria, and you almost made one. She came from a past of unrealistic expectations, and she rejected that utterly and completely. You had your own rejections, the way you saw your family.

You both found familial trauma a thing to bond over.

"I could never return to Dhara," she would often say. "There's nothing for me there."

And you told her how both your parents went to the place your grandfather made habitable, but you didn't because you couldn't bear to live around them, and so you came to this other place, which had nothing to do with your family whatsoever. If you would have said the same thing to literally anyone else, they would have scorned you and come at you with pitchforks.

But not Maria, who respected the sentiment.

With Maria, you made an after and never thought of what came before.

But between your old-before and a new-before, there was Maria and a quiet night in Jherek, an insulated dome-precinct in Serron-Karra. The night sky here is shades of green and purple, particularly nebulous, but not because of atmospheric pollution, rather the opposite, because of gaseous presence way above, and a cluster of stars refracting so much light it eventually transforms into a vast halo.

Maria's head is on your chest, and you're playing with her hair. "Selnor-two is installing a new chaat counter next week," you say to Maria. "Wanna go?" She mumbles something, and you take that as a yes. A small knot of her auburn hair inadvertently ties around your finger, and you try to wrench it away without disturbing her. But she has now gone into a zone of thought it's nigh impossible to pry her out of, unless she really wants to. You wait for her to come out, gradually, while you breathe and watch the sky.

She eventually faces you. Her eyes are red, her lips too. She looks like she has emerged out of a deep dream. You could kiss her, again and again. But you stop yourself. Then, Maria is on top of you, kissing you. You can't contain yourself and kiss her back, even though you've just made out half an hour ago. You can't get enough of her.

When you're done, you ask her about her zone of thought. She wants you to see for yourself, and then you both crawl out of the bed and plug yourselves into the SelfDreamer, where both of you could share a vision.

You've seen this coming a mile away, yet it hits you like a freight train.

Inside the SelfDreamer, you are consumed by Maria's vision for her future. This future has seneschals from Ul-Aria, palgraves from Marren-Kla, and the cursed hessens from Karom-Karra. Her vision has miles upon miles of carmine glades, with no structures, no buildings whatsoever. There's no space for Jherek, Serron-Karra, or you.

Unless you agree, of course.

When you come out of her zone of thought, you pose her this question. Why is she thinking what she is thinking? Aren't they in their perfect place, here inside the cocooned dome of Jherek, where the fifty-third colony of Dhara settlers is just about to arrive. Isn't this a great home away from home, you ask?

No, it's not, because her heart wants what it wants, and it wants to be away because the cocoon is now grating at her every passing day.

You don't remember what you said to her. It must have been something silly. Or something serious. Or it could have been a breaking point. Or just a medley of nothing-words, a jumble. You blame yourself for ruining that moment, and consequently, a life, because you weren't ready.

You were, perhaps, just angry at your inability to change.

You remember that night 'til the hair-knot around your finger, the only thing worth remembering.

But listen.

Your fingers are itching to carve a new truth, a new now, which could later become a new-before. Not immediately, though. Now your fingers are clasped tightly around a briefcase you're tired of carrying. Your stomach is twisting and turning from eating only space food, and you want something substantial. Maybe the remnant of Dhara, the now-empty planet, with a handful of stubborn people who refused to leave, still has great food. You could really use a samosa.

But why are you even here?

You've taken the entrails of this past and coiled them around a dead thing and kicked it to dust. You now know it no more. You don't want to live it. Families are ugly, and that's why you left this place, hated that other place named Karom-Karra, and went to yet another place.

Maria. A broken, uglier whisper.

A year after your breakup with Maria, you make up your mind to return to Dhara. When you were still inside the dome in Jherek, your parents, lightyears away, wondered why you weren't returning to stay with them instead. You told them in as many words as you could muster, whatever truth came out of you, but they wouldn't know how to use the Pipecom Node to transmit their message to you on Serron-Karra. But you know they are thinking along the same lines.

Come to us, Kiki. There's so much greenery here.

You imagine sending a message along the lines of "Karom-Karra has nothing for me," but the word "nothing" comes back to bite you before you even think of sending it. Family can't be nothing, and you would not hear the end of it, 'til the end of time. If you had mentioned *nothing*, every statement of your mother would be tinged with a heaviness, a turgid *something.*

Five weeks later, you hear a broken whisper on the Pipecom Node installed inside Jherek. Vainly, you are expecting to hear Maria's voice from Ul-Aria. *Kiki, I am playing with the seneschals, and I wish you were here.* And you think you'd leave everything and go to Ul-Aria if you got even a hint that she wanted you there.

But instead, the whisper belongs to your dad.

Go visit your grandfather on Dhara if you've made up your mind.

That same way station. Leading to the same dust-clogged skies. Narrow winding roads down below. Touch-me-nots. A home before home before home.

"But why?"

You say into the Pipecom but never send it. You've been asking "why" your entire life. You've been rebelling against this made-up idea of a family your parents hold in their hearts. That's why you came here to start anew. But you're also a coward who can't say what comes to mind. When you actually say it, you break many hearts.

More broken messages arrive in a turgid stream.

He has not been feeling well lately.

We have done our bit for the family. It's time for the next generation to do their bit.

It's not pain you hear in your father's voice. It's the shrugging off of a burden, a relief. You want to say sorry, but you have gone after your mother, and apologies don't come easily to you.

Maria hated that. Pride fucks with you enough for you to apologize. You lost Maria to give a trophy to your pride. Champion of champions.

What did you win?

It's your choice now, a one-of-its-kind trade-off, to return to Dhara for a better now. You don't care for any of those habitable planets in the universe where your own civilization has now spread. But what place are you returning to? A loveless, heartless place, more so than the world you left behind. You saw a rot, left for a garden. But the rot is everywhere. Where, then, are you? You've fought and left behind so many worlds that you're now world-less.

Nomad. Spacie. Wanderer.

But listen.

A voice.

You're wrenched unceremoniously out of the reverie this way station plunged you into. You see a face. A face from your childhood you should probably recognize. The man is standing on the bridge that connects the launchpad to the waiting area, where the empty caves of the space-homeless start.

Instincts kick in, and you prepare to answer in a different language, a language you and Maria perfected together. But the hard lines forming on the man's forehead force you to switch to something more archaic, more formal. It sounds stilted, but the man accepts it.

"Don't you wish you could have arrived on the other Gevesham, the one with the direct view of the pyramids?" he says, while watching you walk through an irradiation and quarantine pipeline. "They've made this entire process much smoother there."

It's embarrassing for you, responding through the glass, but you nod along. You don't even remember the man's name, you just know he's the one who will take you to your grandfather. You wonder if you made the right call, leaving Serron-Karra. You cross many docking stations, one mammoth structure after another, multiple disjointed units working with some sort of cohesion, some fueling, some maintaining gravity, others powering the hyperdrive that sends and receives people. You have seen this process working smoothly and efficiently in the other way station, and you find yourself agreeing to the question posed by the man.

Much, much later, after you've slept a cold sleep and woken up even colder, you find your eyes becoming accustomed to the perennial smoke cloud around you. You are inside another quarantine bunker, this time on earth. So many steps, so many protocols. It wasn't supposed to be this hard, coming back. The man who greeted you is standing outside, you can see his lithe outline as he waits for you to freshen up.

Was this normal? Was this how your grandfather was always greeted? Your memory is fleeting, and you can only see vague shapes of the past instead of remembering incidents. Now you recall how your grandpa always came home two days *after* actually returning. You would see him on the way station because it was a trip for you, and then you would forget it all, until you would see him again, at home, two days later.

Now you know where the two days went. Now you know why you went home first with your mother, while your father stayed back.

The bunker opens with a hiss, and the man who greeted you enters.

"It's time, sirji," he says.

"Call me Kaushal," you say. He purses his lips, then introduces himself. His name is Faisal, and he is the house caretaker, in your absence, your family's absence. Yes, Faisal, of course, you remember now. It's uncanny how a memory gets triggered inside your brain at the mention of a mere name. Faisal, who took you to see your first tadpole.

"The situation is dire at home. Babuji has stopped eating and drinking completely."

And somehow, you are supposed to mend that. What are you going to do? This is a grown-up situation.

You step inside Faisal's jeep. It trudges along what's now a skeleton of a road, surrounded by thick weeds and other wild things. You try to look behind what you've left, but you really can't because the smoke is just too much. What was the quarantine bunker connected to? A space elevator? An aircraft that took you above to the Gevesham? When you were small, it was definitely an aircraft, but again, those memories are now just shapes.

"Do you have plans of returning to Karom-Karra?"

"I . . . I came from Serron-Karra," you say.

"Oh, I thought you would be staying with Lalitaji and Sumitji."

Your face is now red from secondhand embarrassment, and your chest feels tight and heavy. Faisal has spent his entire life committed to one man, one duty, and can't imagine independence, so you don't think much of his question.

But you think of other things.

Like how you are just a boy.

Once, a boy from Dhara, who was chasing tadpoles beside a pond. Then a boy who became a man, a Charter, the scribe who traveled to Serron-Karra to write about how it was still the perfect land for human settlement. You wrote papers that became foundational cornerstones for sustainable farming in other lands, so people could get access to real food and not space gloop. The boy who fell in love.

Now, you come back, and you think you're a copy of the boy who left Dhara. Is the copy of a boy another boy, or does the process add or subtract something, you think.

Being just a boy is a bad thing. That's what they tell you, drill in you. But are you? Maria called you a boy. A little boy inside a little boy inside a big boy inside a man. A Russian doll of little boys. She called you a boy out of love. Your family calls you a boy out of pity. In the end, you're left seething. Because none of them are really yours anymore.

But listen.

Listen to the susurrus of the wind when you reach the place you called a summer home in childhood. An echo from the past. A wrought iron gate, behind which there's a verandah, home to numerous touch-me-nots and lilies. The outside walls are the same as you'd remembered, albeit freshly painted.

You walk the stone-peppered trail inside, and remembrance smacks you in the face. The house is the same. Except, it seems much smaller now. Prohibitively smaller. Of course it feels that way. The house that exists in your memory is the experience of a six year old. Now, you're twenty-six. Twenty years have shrunk the house twenty times. And you feel yourself shrinking to occupy the space better.

You see a thin figure lying on a charpai, once a man who wore the uniform of the space-cadets who went in search of Karom-Karra, now a forgotten thing, mottled and dying. Language eludes you in that moment, and your mouth could only form vague shapes. A sigh, a groan.

But the old man turns and looks at you with his deep, gray eyes.

"Kiki, you've come home," he says.

Kiki, he says, not Kuku. He's not a copy of a copy, and you're yourself. You can make this your truth, again, your *now.* So when, later, this now becomes your before, you can say you did well. The Russian doll is opening with a crack.

Are you listening?

ABOUT THE AUTHOR

Amal Singh is an author from Mumbai, India. His short fiction has been longlisted for the BSFA award, and has appeared or is forthcoming in numerous venues such as *Tor.com, Clarkesworld, F&SF, Apex, Asimov's,* among others. His debut novel, *The Garden of Delights* is now out from Flame Tree Press.

Hunter Harvester

BAM BRUIN

Bunch, you'll be able to find most of this in the official reports. Considering what we learned that day, there will be plenty of them. But let me tell you what happened, how it was for me. You, of all people, should want to hear it.

It was morning still, when the doctor told me about you, just before she got called away for some minor emergency. The examination room suddenly felt too small. I began to breathe hard and felt my heart beat fast. I quickly zipped up my coveralls and peeked out to see where the doctor had gone, then moved fast in the other direction. Keeping quiet, I exited the medical dome. Outside, I leaned against the next dome and for a moment tasted only Baber's sweet air—and whatever was coming up my throat.

I panicked, wanted to keep moving. When I saw a large rover start up across the town square, I got out in front and waved it down. The rover duly stopped, swaying a little on its six giant wheels, and Revazova peeked out the window. She frowned as I climbed the ladder but held the door open for me.

"Where to?" I asked, trying to smile as I drew level with her.

"Cabbage hunt," she answered with a shrug.

"I'll lend a hand," I said, getting in. But I froze when I saw the rover's one other passenger. Hwang. Always so certain, always ready to make the right decision. She looked at me as I took a seat, then turned away with a short nod and set the rover back on its way with a few taps on its control screen.

"Every chance you'll get to find a Folder, huh?" Revazova shook her head at me. "Anyone else, and I'd wonder if they'd gone crazy. Volunteering for a hunt . . . "

“Doesn’t calling it a hunt make it more exciting?” I jabbed back. Still, I was grateful for Revazova’s habit of making quick assumptions, for a change. It saved me the effort of having to explain myself. She wasn’t stupid, of course: I *had* been tagging along with about every vehicle that might come near the forests. Back when we arrived, and Baber was still full of unknowns, our landing site in the middle of a wide-open area made sense. But as a biologist, and the only one specialized in behavior instead of biochemistry, I needed to be in the forests. That’s where we found the Folders.

Less exciting but no less important, the forests are also where the cabbages grow. We were far behind schedule in growing any Earth crop in meaningful amounts. Miraculously, the cabbages cover our every nutritional need—and they didn’t even taste half bad. We’d been surviving on them since our stores ran low. Their only downside appeared to be the long trips back and forth to the forests to harvest them.

“Thank you for helping out,” Hwang said when she was done plotting the rover’s route. She turned her seat around, and if her gaze normally made me feel like I let her down, this morning it made me *burn* with guilt. Hwang was currently Leader, a natural in that role, and had held the position multiple times before. My throat felt pinched, and I replied with only a grunt as I opened a window.

The rover had left the domes behind and picked up speed on the rolling hills. I stuck out my hand to feel the breeze that rippled through the blue and yellow flyflower fields. The silver-green sun was already warm, glittering in the scattered ponds. When the rover slowed down to crest a hill, I could see a single flyflower reach out above the others, its blue petals fluttering to reveal a furry, segmented body inside. Soon it tore itself loose from trailing, withered roots and found its stride. The newly born flowerfly soared away on the breeze, and for a moment, I forgot everything but the sheer joy of being on this strange planet full of wonderful life.

Folders are most wonderful of all, Bunch, but the balloontree forests themselves come a close second. From a distance, they look like any young growth forest back on Earth, all those thin trunks reaching high before maturing, leaves perched at the top. But Baber balloontrees can grow to be a thousand feet high, and most are in the high hundreds. Those thin yellow trunks shouldn’t be able to carry all that tree, and really, they don’t. Hidden among the foliage at the top are huge bladders full of lighter-than-air gases keeping it all aloft. The forests are a sight to behold, always daunting to approach, but my sense of vertigo had never been as strong as on that day.

The rover slowed down at the forest edge where its tall wheels went from crushing flyflowers to sinking deep into the layers of fallen balloontree leaves, curled long and yellow bright on top of wet, fertile mulch. Not fertile enough for Earth crops, we had learned.

Leaning out the window, I breathed in the deep humus smell and wondered what the ground lacked. Our own personal "seed" certainly wasn't affected here on Baber. Fifty percent of fertilized ova developed into viable fetuses, just like back on Earth. A one in two chance that I felt right there in my throat.

I was glad we quickly found a cabbage patch to take my mind off things. Hwang switched the rover to manual drive and expertly backed up its cargo bed. The nearly perfectly round, dark red cabbages made me realize I'd skipped breakfast that morning.

"Isn't that a Folder?" Revazova pointed, instantly making me forget my hunger again.

"Yes!" I raced down the ladder, sinking deep into the mulch when I jumped down the last steps. I set off for the tree where the Folder sat and soon heard the others' feet squelch behind me.

"Those must be this one's cabbages," Hwang said, trying to catch up.

"Not necessarily," I called out over my shoulder, "I've seen them right next to a patch, completely disinterested. Like when I took that first cabbage, remember? One of them even seemed to encourage me."

"How can you tell a Folder is *encouraging*?" Revazova asked as she drew up beside me.

"It's . . . " I faltered. "I just . . . know . . . I spend so much time with them. They're social, just like us . . . Hold it." I put a hand on Revazova's shoulder to keep her back. Even though we were close enough for the Folder to notice us, it kept its long back to us, sitting up straight, twenty feet of bony spine stretching skin under short, gray fur.

"I didn't know you discovered the cabbages," Revazova said, then shrugged. "Makes sense."

"Discover? I just brought one back when I saw an opportunity—"

"What's it doing?" Hwang cut me off as she reached us.

"Maybe nothing," I said, slowly circling around. The Folder sat on its four hind limbs, but the oddly triangular segments of its other limbs were moving quickly, bone and tendon flashing beneath the fur. All those joints have a habit of settling in different positions continuously. But this was something else . . . "It's carving!"

In my excitement, I raised my voice enough for the Folder to finally take notice. It turned toward me with that friendly face stuck between the folds of its forelimbs, big black eyes and mouth curled in a Mona Lisa smile. For all their size, Folders had never made a threatening move toward humans, and those faces reassured me every time. Within seconds, it turned back to the balloontree, and curls of bark began to fly again.

"I've *never* seen a Folder carve before," I told the others, so worked up I kept clenching and spreading my hands.

"But you must have recorded hundreds of carvings. I've seen them," Hwang stage-whispered, making her sound even more insistent than usual.

"Yes. I already concluded it makes them tool-users, as well as social and intelligent," I said, "and now, I can finally *see* those tools."

"I don't think you could call them tools," Revazova's dry voice came from the other side of the Folder. I joined her there, and my heart sank as I saw what the Folder used to cut those graceful, complex loops into the amber wood glowing below the yellow bark.

"Like a nail, or a single claw, on each limb," Hwang said, then turned to me. "You've never seen those before? Are they usually retracted?"

"Just scratchings," Revazova waved dismissively.

"*Just scratchings?* They study each other's carvings, you know. Some carvings are high up a tree, which means they must have been carved decades, centuries ago. There has to be so much in them, narratives at least, stories maybe, morals . . . We'll be busy trying to understand them for years—" I stopped when I turned and saw Revazova had gone back to the cabbage patch. Hwang still listened to me, but now she looked at the Folder, and her eyes suddenly grew wide. A sudden rush of air passed me. The Folder was between the cabbage patch and Revazova in seconds.

Once there, it simply sat back down and looked at her with its friendly face.

"It's different, knowing it has those claws . . . " Revazova said when we met her back at the rover.

It was darker, deeper in the forest, the silver taken out of the sunlight, leaving only the green to float down with the balloontree leaves. The rover came to a complete standstill every now and then, to calculate a route it could fit among the trunks that stood ever closer together. The going was slow. In the aftermath of the earlier encounter, I felt free enough to ask Hwang why we didn't circle the more open, outer parts of the forest. She said it had been getting harder to find cabbage patches.

"I hadn't noticed," I told her.

"You don't notice much, outside your own research project, do you?" A smile flashed across her face.

"I . . . maybe . . . " I turned away, my cheeks burning again. But anger seeped through the guilt this time. I looked back at her. "Why did we start the pregnancy program when we're still unsure about where our next meal comes from?"

"We have to think of ourselves on Baber *long-term*," Hwang said with no trace of her smile left. "In any case, we don't really have to worry about food."

"Just one cabbage hunt is enough to keep us all fed for ten days," Revazova added, lying back on her seat.

"It just doesn't feel like the right time to start taking care of a baby." I said it quietly, but just then the rover stopped again, and the words rang loud in the deep forest.

"We'll *all* take care of *all* babies," Revazova finally said, sitting up.

"Then why do we *all* need to have them?"

"There are ninety-seven of us, and they couldn't have fitted one more person on that starcraft. Ninety-seven of us to build something that lasts on this planet. It's easy enough to freeze sperm and ova, but only our wombs can turn them into the next generation," Hwang said, patiently, as if she read the lines from a projection on the inside of her skull.

"Then why not send a hundred teenagers and force *them* to breed," I snapped.

"Because we're scientists, engineers, the most talented and skilled people they could find. That's why we had a chance of settling here in the first place, survive what we encounter, understand this strange planet. We are the best humanity has to offer," Hwang said, raising her hand to keep me from interrupting, her voice firm, "and that includes our reproductive health. It's the only way to make it here on Baber, and you should know all this. You signed the contract."

"That contract was the only way to make it *to* Baber," I said and stared out at balloontree leaves landing dry and brittle on the damp ground while the rover slowly set off again.

"No wonder Folders don't give a shit about these," Revazova said as we lifted the fourth or fifth cabbage onto the rover's little lift. "They're a bit small, aren't they?"

We'd checked the area thoroughly when we finally found this cabbage patch, circling it first in the rover and then on foot, and found no trace of any Folders.

"Their roots are almost gone already," Hwang added from atop the cargo bed where she stacked the cabbages.

"We don't actually know *why* the Folders protect some cabbages and don't care for others," I told them.

"Well," Revazova said, "wouldn't you rather eat the big, juicy, purple ones we saw before?"

"Sure," I said, feeling hungry again. "But as far as I know, Folders don't eat them."

"What?" Revazova looked up in surprise, almost dropping the next cabbage.

"They're omnivores, aren't they?" Hwang asked, puzzled.

"Sure." I shrugged. "Whatever that means on Baber. We've seen them eat anything from deflated balloontree bladders to flowerflies."

"But *not* the cabbages, of all things?"

"Never observed."

"Then how did you figure out they were edible in the first place?" Revazova frowned at the few cabbages left on the withered root bed.

"As I tried to tell you before, that wasn't me. I just brought one back when I saw the opportunity to do so. It was Hwang who decided to analyze them as a foodstuff. And credit where credit is due. They'll feed generations to come—as long as we keep finding enough of them."

The harvest didn't quite fill up the cargo bed, but it was still heavy enough for the rover to sink even deeper into the mulch, slowing us down yet further on the way out of the forest. Revazova leaned back and closed her eyes, but Hwang kept throwing furtive glances at me. I stared outside again to avoid them—stared hard enough to notice a far-off spot of purple, impossibly bright among the muted greens and yellows. It felt as if the forest wanted to assure us, Bunch, as if it wanted to tell us all those generations to come would be alright. But when we reached the patch, there were only a few cabbages.

"At least that big one on the left looks really ripe," Revazova said, up and about as quickly as she'd fallen asleep before. Most of the vines in the root bed still looked fresh, but across them lay only shriveled remains, loose, paper-thin cabbage leaves that disintegrated at a touch.

"I've seen patches like these. They're usually under Folder care," I said, looking around.

"Let's check out the area," Hwang said, but Revazova groaned.

"We're still so close to that last patch," she said, "we searched that whole place! Come on. There weren't any Folders there, there won't be any here."

We compromised and left the rover behind to each make a ten-minute loop on foot. In the forest on my own, it was quiet enough to hear the doctor's voice again, telling me what she told me that morning. But my panic was cut short when a sudden *crack* cut through from above. I looked up to see a balloontree bladder tear loose from its branch and quickly rise. A sharp silver sunbeam shot through the gap, and I thought of you, Bunch. The bladders hold the balloontrees' seed, and this one might land somewhere to grow a thousand feet tall—or it might be eaten by a passing Folder.

"Maybe something's wrong with these cabbages, something we can't see," Revazova said after we returned. "Something in the soil?"

"We'll ask Sanger's team to run a few extra tests," Hwang nodded.

"Hope she'll have the time," I said, "she got pregnant from the first round of inseminations, didn't she?"

Hwang shot me a look, but before she could say anything, Revazova called us over to help with the big cabbage. It took all three of us to get it on the rover's lift. Atop the cargo bed, it nearly rolled away before Revazova managed to secure it in a corner. In awe of her strength, Hwang and I both reached for Revazova's biceps at the same time, and we all laughed. It was a relief to have a full harvest, and we quickly got inside the rover to set it on its way home. For a moment, the wheels slipped underneath us, and we feared the weight had become too much. But then they found some purchase among the leaves with a shock that set the rover swaying and us all laughing again. The rover picked its deliberate path, and the forest became lighter, the trees farther apart, the ground firmer. Then we burst out onto the bright flyflower fields, picking up speed while clods of dense mulch flew off from between the wheels' ridges.

"By the way," Revazova said, "It's been about three months, and the doctor says all's well."

"*You're* pregnant?" I blurted out.

"Is that so strange?" Revazova laughed.

"No . . . of course . . . " I caught myself. "But . . . you were lifting those cabbages all by yourself!"

"Yeah, yeah, don't worry." She waved dismissively. "I'm not stupid. I'll notice if it's too much of a strain."

"Congratulations," Hwang said with a quick smile, putting her hand on Revazova's shoulder.

"Thanks. I'm pretty stoked, to be honest. And so's Cay: she really looks forward to playing with the little brat." Revazova grinned, flushing.

"See," I said, "*that's* what a child should have . . . "

The others looked at me oddly, but before they could say anything, a loud, sudden sound reverberated through the rover. It appeared to make no impression on the rover itself, but Hwang quickly stopped it to see if we'd hit anything. There was nothing to find but crushed flyflowers and the aniseed smell coming off their broken petals.

"It's that big cabbage," Revazova called down after she climbed up the cargo bed, motioning for us to join her. The cabbage wasn't secure among the smaller ones anymore, and a few of its outer leaves had come off. We pushed it back, puzzled about what could have caused it to move during the smooth ride.

"What's *that*?" Hwang pointed in the direction we'd come from.

"Something's kicking up a whole lot of flyflowers," Revazova put her hand over her eyes and peered into the distance.

"They're *Folders*," I said, squinting.

"Are they moving very fast?" Revazova asked.

"It's strange," I said, uncertain, "I thought they didn't like direct sunlight—I've only ever seen them outside the forests after dusk."

"Are they headed . . . straight for us?" Hwang asked, and we searched the gentle hills stretching featureless in each direction for some other destination for the rushing Folders.

"Probably best to get out of their way," I said, and we hurried back inside. But even before the rover reached its cruising speed, we heard another sound just like the first.

"It's that big one again," Hwang said. "But . . . how?"

"Yeah, OK," Revazova called, sticking her head out of the window to look back, "but let's move away from those animals first!"

"Folders aren't just *animals*," I snapped.

"Well," Revazova shot back, "they move a little fast for plants, don't they?"

"Alright, we'll look at that cabbage later," Hwang said, switching the rover to manual and making a sharp turn. Miraculously, the whole harvest stayed on board. But as soon as we straightened out, I could see the big cabbage move again. It rolled and shoved the smaller cabbages . . . Movements that looked unnatural. Or rather, deliberate. In my mind, I heard Revazova again—and then it struck me.

"Slow down," I told Hwang. "Stop the rover!"

Does it seem obvious now, Bunch, when you read this? Maybe we'd been too hungry to think clearly. I sure had other things on my mind at the time, or one thing, really. Which was you, of course.

Cabbages aren't just cared for by Folders. Cabbages *are* Folders.

Like that big, purple cabbage we'd taken, tumbling around our rover. We cowered inside while the Folders chasing us took it off the cargo bed, and between their many limbs, we could see it *unfold*. It really looks a lot like a flyflower turning into a flowerfly.

The root beds with all those tangled vines aren't just there for the cabbages to soak up the nutrients from the forest floor: they connect to each other. Through them, to the biochemists' enormous excitement, their DNA is exchanged. After that complicated cross-fertilization, about half the patches produce offspring. It's the same fifty-fifty chance the doctor had given my womb earlier that morning. Just a bunch of cells, for now, she'd said, and that's where I got your name, Bunch.

We've already learned that the Folders *choose* what patches to care for, and those are most often the patches where cabbages keep developing, and eventually, unfolding. The cabbages that do develop take the nutrients from those that don't, through the root vines. Plenty of patches remain without developing cabbages, and so, full of nutrients. It's those patches the Folders let us harvest. I'm still convinced they even encourage us to eat those cabbages.

But not everyone was happy to learn what we've been eating. Hwang has dedicated as much of our capabilities as possible to the production of alternative food sources. Part of that is that she's granted a hold on inseminations for everyone who prefers to keep working.

In the end, it wasn't time for you yet either, Bunch. But I'll keep your name, for if and when you do come. That'll be up to chance and choice, as with all life everywhere.

ABOUT THE AUTHOR

Bam Bruin is a European writer who also works as a traffic controller for the local subway. Bam loves soil life on this planet and any other, is obsessed by the French Revolution, cries for old forests dying, and tries to read and write stories and a novel about all of it at the same time.

Wilderness Resurrection and Compromise

PRIYA SRIDHAR

Humans have a gift for wiping out predatory species. Fear and misunderstanding sometimes motivate these decisions, and by the time we realize our mistake, it's often too late. Those with power in their hands often refuse to admit they did something wrong, and the United States is still a primary sponsor of trophy hunting and hunting animals for sport. That often means we must work around the decision-makers, negotiate, put in safeguards, or constantly remind the perpetrators of their inhumane destruction.

We also don't have a definite answer on one important issue: reintroducing species to their natural environments after reinvigorating dwindling or very small numbers. Clashes with existing species and humans and new ones are always emerging, like a species of the cloud tiger cat in South America. Though they are shy and avoid humans, habitat destruction and interested trophy hunters threaten them. The same goes for many other species we haven't identified yet. And what about our desire to bring back those that have gone extinct?

A Clone Cacophony

In April 2025, a company named Colossal Biosciences claimed to bring back the dire wolf, a species that died out ten thousand years ago. New Scientist has confirmed this is not the case; the dire wolf and gray wolf last had a common ancestor six million years ago. In fact, "the two species share 99.5 percent of their DNA. Since the gray wolf genome is around 2.4 billion base pairs" (Le Page 2025), that means 120 million base pairs are different between the two species. To create the three cubs, Colossal Biosciences made twenty gene edits. Editing gray wolf DNA to "resurrect" the dire wolf would require far more edits and need accurate predictions for any potential mutation.

The actual work they're doing to help species restoration would help endangered ones; per Yahoo News, "Colossal scientists hope to use what they've learned to help the endangered red 'ghost' wolf, which has a very limited gene pool remaining" (Hayes 2025). Using gene editing to increase diversity within a species and reduce the long-term hazards of inbreeding would assist many slow-breeding animals.

There is also the big question: what do we do when the extinction is reversed? How do we handle backlash from interested decision-makers like farmers, ranchers, poachers, trophy hunters, influencers, and loggers?

The first solution that comes to mind is creating zoos and preserves with controlled environments. Science fiction, however, has told us that humans are not very good at zoology with extinct species. Our cinematic counterparts *never* listen to the experts.

"Welcome to Jurassic Park!"

Both the novel and film versions of Michael Crichton's classic show the consequences of not managing a properly controlled environment for extinct species. In both cases, Dr. John Hammond tries to create a dinosaur zoo where the herbivores would "wow" the target demographic, and the carnivores would scare them. Certain species of dinosaur are much larger or smarter than the humans viewing them. Large ones can trample the guests, while the smaller and sometimes smarter carnivores can trap anyone unlucky enough to end up in their sights. Dr. Hammond, Dr. Henry Wu, and head engineer, Ray Arnold, all believe electric fences and a single game warden, Robert Muldoon, will keep the park under control.

Enter one of our protagonists, Dr. Ian Malcolm. The book version of Malcolm uses chaos theory to explain that the park has too many unknown variables to guarantee guest safety. In the movie, Malcolm says that Hammond hasn't thought through all the worst-case possibilities when featuring a park with extinct dinosaurs and scoffs that the Jurassic Park managers are wielding genetic force "like your dad's gun" (Spielberg 1993). This sentiment is expertly demonstrated in the infamous steer feeding scene, and though our Drs. Malcolm, Sattler, and Grant don't actually see the dinosaurs, they see what remains of the live lunch that was lowered into the enclosure.

No one can ignore Muldoon reporting that the velociraptors are whacking themselves against the fence to test for weak spots. The audience may already feel uneasy that Muldoon failed to save an employee from a velociraptor in the film's opening. Hearing his confirmation that they want to escape and that they prefer violence? It should send ice down our spines.

Malcolm further chastises those involved in this project, who bank on both the "wow factor" and the promise of quick money without plans for long-term conservation. " . . . I'll tell you the problem with the scientific power that you're using here, it didn't require any discipline to attain it. You read what others had done and you took the next step. You didn't earn the knowledge for yourselves, so you don't take any responsibility for it . . . " (Spielberg 1993).

The park is also missing one critical type of employee: a zoologist. Sure, there's a veterinarian on staff, but zoology is a whole different ballpark. Per Unity University (2021), "A zoologist studies animals both in the wild and captivity. By observing various species in their habitats, zoologists understand how animals behave in the wild. Their goal is to identify and monitor how different species interact within their ecosystem." A zoologist can use these observations and scientific research to design an ideal environment.

Part of the reason the dinosaurs rampage is that they lack a mentally stimulating and nurturing environment. Rexy, as people have nick-named the female T-Rex, doesn't have any giant toys or enrichment activities to occupy her time. Her enclosure only has tied-up goats for food. That's it. It's no wonder that when she sees the cars and a flashlight that shines directly into her eyes that she mistakes the kids' Jeep for a threat to her territory. We probably don't have to detail the boredom of the velociraptors that don't have any toys or exercises that stimulate them, considering how rapidly they go on the attack. In Jurassic Park, the *guests* are the toys. The *guests* are the stimulation.

What's interesting is that within this franchise, the main company that owned Jurassic Park learned from some of its mistakes. In *Jurassic World*, InGen management hires military dolphin trainer Owen Grady to work with their new batch of velociraptors. Grady raises the pack from birth, socializes them, and imprints on them. He uses clicker training for enrichment and negotiation so that if things go wrong, the raptors are less likely to eat a guest or park employee. While to outsiders it looks like Grady has complete control of a situation, he says, "I don't control the raptors. It's a relationship. It's based on mutual respect" (Trevorrow 2018). He doesn't recommend showing them to the public, let alone the military. The raptors like him but will attack if they have an off day or decide that Grady is no longer the alpha. Later on, when the pack chooses a new leader, Owen focuses on keeping his coworker, Claire, and her nephews alive rather than reasoning with the pack until he has no choice. The raptors are sapient beings with intellect and rapid reflexes, and they are not dramatic pets.

Off the silver screen, a similar plan and thought process must come sooner rather than later. Colossal Biosciences is also working on bringing back the Tasmanian tiger from extinction. It seems like a good idea considering how many Tasmanian residents would like this to happen; bar owner Doug Westbrook in Mole Creek, the last place with an official search, believes he saw one. Such a resurrection could be an act of atonement for the poster child of human-wrought damage; in the wrong hands, though, it could also lead to trauma for the cloned creatures.

What Happened to the Tasmanian Tiger?

Europeans. Europeans came to Australia. They introduced sheep, foxes, cane toads, rabbits, and other invasive species. As Thomas Dunlap put it, none too delicately, "The story of whites and the natural environment of Australia is the tale of a European culture in a non-European land" (Dunlap 1993). Settlers wanted to change the continent with farming and development rather than adapt to the various biomes.

Also known as the Tasmanian wolf, the marsupial wolf, or the thylacine, the Tasmanian tiger was an apex predator. The "tiger" part came from stripes on their back, one way to identify them. According to Greg Heberle, however, they weren't pack animals like *Canis* wolf species; in fact, "They usually hunted alone or in pairs, or small family groups of up to two adults and four young, preying on kangaroos, wallabies, small animals, and birds" (Heberle 2004). They also avoided humans as much as possible, being "shy and secretive."

The European settlers, unwilling to accept that Tasmanian biomes hated their farming approach, blamed local predators. When a photograph showing a Tasmanian tiger carrying a chicken emerged in 1921, ranchers latched onto the fear that this monstrous beast would eat up their birds. However, under further scrutiny nearly 84 years later, it was concluded that the photograph had been doctored to elicit that exact response. It was discovered that the beast in question was actually in a caged environment and hadn't "come out of the wild to raid a hen house" (Freeman 2005). Humans just needed an excuse to act.

Colonizers within Australia encouraged the hunting of the apex predators: "The Government-introduced bounty scheme from 1888–1909 was paid on more than 2200 thylacines" (Heberle 2004). By the time that any conservationists could have saved the Tasmanian tigers, it was too late; the last one died in the Hobart Zoo in 1936.

Of course, you may be asking the obvious question: what about species in captivity? Turns out that thylacines didn't adapt to captivity well. They also were slow breeders, having only one litter a year with two or three cubs.

Surely, though, international zoos would have the resources and equipment to maintain breeding programs. We have seen them keep other endangered species like Bengal tigers alive and announce the births with joy. Unfortunately for the Tasmanian tiger, they didn't live in an age with trained wildlife veterinarians, airplane accommodations, regular tranquilizers, and quarantines. They had to deal with the stress of captivity and transport with nineteenth century veterinary care.

What does that mean? Many Tasmanian tiger bodies were sold to taxidermists, and no breeding program ensued. Most didn't survive trips to London despite a high demand: "The long sea journey was harsh and many of the thylacines shipped from Van Diemen's land were simply declared 'dead on arrival.' One animal died just eight days after arriving in 1888" (Edmonds and Stark 2018). If pairs were shipped, one Tasmanian tiger would most likely perish, rendering the whole process futile.

The number of dead that remain is haunting. As Penny Edmonds and Hannah Stark write, "Some 167 specimens of Tasmanian tigers reside in museums in the UK alone." Humans around the world have recorded footage of the last Tasmanian tiger in Hobart Zoo, along with pelts, skeletons, and stuffed bodies.

None of these are equivalent to the life of the species lost. We humans failed the Tasmanian tiger; the same goes for the passenger pigeon, the toolache wallaby, the Florida black wolf, and *hundreds* of other species. A resurrection could provide our chance to make things right. We just have to add the "how" of future zoology to go with the Lazarus-styled cloning.

How Can We Resurrect a Species Lost a Hundred Years Ago?

NPR questioned how Colossal Biosciences obtained the DNA necessary for their Tasmanian tiger project. Mosquitoes preserved in amber cannot provide those raw materials in real life; Andrew Pask recounts that the taxidermal bodies actually gave the company their lucky break. He and his team found a baby Tasmanian tiger preserved in ethanol, as well as the mother's skinned head: "Despite the thing looking pretty gruesome, it's actually an incredibly well-preserved specimen that had really intact DNA, which was fantastic for our ability to build a genome" (Daniel 2004). The baby also contains RNA, which is useful for identifying authentic physical features. They then found the Tasmanian tiger's closest living relative and used analytical AI to edit the genome.

The reintroduction itself, however, would be the hard part. The world has changed since 1936, with a larger human population and reduced habitats in native lands. Tasmania and Australia would both have to approve a reintroduction program, with lobbyists and special interest groups undoubtedly providing their two cents. If the Tasmanian tigers are no longer shy, they may appear as a threat to the 2020s farmers and ranchers. Not to mention there would be tourists and locals seeking them out to witness such a miracle.

So, How Do We Omnivores Live with Reintroduced Carnivores?

First, we need to hire experts and listen to them. Put room in your budget for zoologists, veterinarians, and so forth.

Second, educate concerned livestock ranchers and farmers. If the decision-makers with guns and money know that these apex predators are not a threat, they can access the tools that allow for stronger fences with deep supports and appropriate repellents. We see this happening already in real life with giant herbivores and carnivores alike. For example, Kenyan farmers use native bee fences and boxes to ward away elephants interested in their crops. It turns into a win-win situation where produce avoids devastation, fields get pollinated, farmers can sell the resulting honey, and no human or elephant gets hurt.

Third, we need technology that does not rely on grant funding or governmental support. Zoos currently fund a large portion of conservation and breeding programs. That means we need nonpartisan zoos with protections from politicians and hunters that fancy themselves going on an African safari. Drones with batteries and camera streams that last for centuries could be a game-changer for monitoring species and anticipating human-related conflicts. The same goes for satellite tracking, radio tags, QR codes, and stable isotopes.

What tools from science fiction could also assist? Perhaps programming different plants or fungi to alert zoologists in the case of illegal habitat destruction or hunting. Conservation could potentially rely on remote robotic veterinary centers that are able to provide point-of-care treatment with real remote vets on call, or nanotechnology MRI devices that self-repair between scans and diagnoses. New possibilities are always being dreamed up and invented as science fiction hits the shelves.

Beyond Taxidermy and Gene Editing

Humans have a responsibility to collaborate and coexist with both each other and those species we resurrect from erasure. We must want to build a better future despite self-interested billionaires who do not understand long-term consequences. To do that, we need to embrace the *Jurassic Park* idiom: "life finds a way," with or without humanity. It also means to turn away from the cool, the wow, and the money-making factors, bridging our destructive past into a prosperous and cooperative future.

If we want to prevent a real-life *Jurassic Park* disaster or at least ensure that any cloned animals will maintain a decent quality of life within their environments, we also need to trust the experts.

References

AZA Staff. 2019. "How Zoos and Aquariums Protect Endangered Species." *Association of Zoos & Aquariums*, March 15, 2019. www.aza.org/connect-stories/stories/how-do-zoos-help-animals

"Trophy Hunting - Born Free USA." *Born Free USA*. 2018. www.bornfreeusa.org/campaigns/wildlife-trade/trophy-hunting/

Dalton, Jane. 2020. "Dentist Who Slaughtered Cecil the Lion 'Hunts and Kills Protected Wild Ram' Just Four Years Later." *The Independent*, July 12, 2020. www.the-independent.com/news/world/asia/walter-palmer-cecil-lion-hunt-ram-sheep-mongolia-a9613856.html

Daniel, Ari. 2024. "Scientists May Be Able to Revive the Tasmanian Tiger from Extinction. But Should They?" *NPR*, October 27, 2024. www.npr.org/2024/10/27/nx-s1-5165198/scientists-may-be-able-to-revive-the-tasmanian-tiger-from-extinction-but-should-they

Dunlap, Thomas R. 1993. "Australian Nature, European Culture: Anglo Settlers in Australia." *Environmental History Review* 17, no. 1, (1993), 25–48. doi.org/10.2307/3984889

Edmonds, Penny, and Hannah Stark. 2018. "Friday Essay: On the Trail of the London Thylacines." *The Conversation*, April 5, 2018.

theconversation.com/friday-essay-on-the-trail-of-the-london-thylacines-91473

Freeman, Carol. 2005. "Is This Picture Worth a Thousand Words? An Analysis of Harry Burrell's Photograph of a Thylacine with a Chicken." *Australian Zoologist* 33, no. 1 (2005), 1–15. doi.org/10.7882/AZ.2005.001

Hale, Tom. 2024. "New Species of Super-Cute Tiger Cat Discovered with an Uncertain Future." *IFLScience*, April 15, 2024. www.iflscience.com/new-species-of-super-cute-tiger-cat-discovered-with-an-uncertain-future-73812

Hayes, Jana. 2025. "Dire Wolves Have Been "Resurrected": See How Scientists Used Ancient DNA to Create the Pups." *Yahoo News*, April 8, 2025. www.yahoo.com/news/dire-wolves-resurrected-see-scientists-193122844.html

Heberle, Greg. 2004. "Reports of Alleged Thylacine Sightings in Western Australia." *Conservation Science Western Australia* 5, no. 1 (2004),1–5. cdn.nimbo.com.au/assets/9e3cfc48eccf81a0d576/8877ce3284b743aefde80ff/uploads/WA_thyla_sightings.pdf

Jolley, Mary Ann. 2023. "Can Scientists Resurrect the Tasmanian Tiger?" *Al Jazeera*, January 29, 2023. www.aljazeera.com/features/2023/1/29/back-from-extinction-resurrecting-the-tasmanian-tiger

Le Page, Michael. 2025. "No, the Dire Wolf Has Not Been Brought Back from Extinction." *New Scientist*, April 7, 2025. www.newscientist.com/article/2475407-no-the-dire-wolf-has-not-been-brought-back-from-extinction/

Spielberg, Steven, dir. 1993. *Jurassic Park*. Universal Pictures.

Tomma, Gennaro. 2025. "Elephants hate bees – here's why that's good news for Kenyan farmers." *BBC*, March 21, 2025. www.bbc.com/future/article/20250320-how-bees-are-reducing-conflict-between-humans-and-elephants

Trevorrow, Colin, et al. 2018. *Jurassic World*. Universal Studios Home Entertainment.

Unity College. 2021. "How to Become a Zoologist." *Unity College*. 2021. unity.edu/careers/zoologist/

ABOUT THE AUTHOR

A 2016 MBA graduate and published author, **Priya Sridhar** has been writing fantasy and science fiction for fifteen years, and counting. She is the author of the Powered series, *Carousel*, *Neo-Mecha Mayhem*, *Understudies*, and many short stories. Priya lives in Miami, Florida with her family.

Who Owns A Story: An Interview with Allison King

ARLEY SORG

Allison King grew up in New Jersey and spent many summers in Taiwan, where she'd visit her cousin. "At first, we role-played some of our favorite stories, such as playing the hares in Redwall. Then we started writing our own stories and fan fiction." Over the years, they continued to send each other stories, which was very likely the seed of a career in writing.

King went to Swarthmore, which was forty-five minutes from her hometown. She majored in engineering, focusing on computer engineering, thinking she'd work in hardware. But it turned out that the English classes were the ones she enjoyed the most. "There was a great Tolkien & Pullman class, and one on Asian American literature that really had a great impact on me. I took my first creative writing workshop my senior year. The engineering requirements made it so there were few opportunities to take other classes, but I really treasure the ones I did take."

After college, Allison King wanted to "venture out a bit . . . my first job was kind of an in-between hardware and software role at MIT Lincoln Laboratory." She developed more software skills and eventually transitioned to focusing primarily on software. She then worked at Cortico, a nonprofit based out of the MIT Media Lab whose mission Allison described as "amplifying underheard voices via deep community conversations." Working at Cortico was the first job that merged her interest in technology with her love of storytelling, a job she held longer than any other. She went from Cortico to Ethyca, a data privacy start-up, "where my claim to fame is having worked on the cookie banner that pops up on *The New York Times*' website in the EU. Although I love the idea of data privacy, I didn't enjoy the for-profit start-up life." Next, she worked at another nonprofit, one that also came out of the MIT Media Lab: Knowledge Futures.

King's fiction career kicked off with "Eden," published in *Flash Fiction Magazine* (July 2019). "Breath of the Dragon King" was published in the October 2021 issue of *Fantasy Magazine*. Her *Fantasy* piece received glowing reviews and was reprinted in Paula Guran's anthology *The Year's Best Fantasy: Volume One* (Pyr, 2022).Micro-fiction "And Again, We Try" appeared in *If There's Anyone Left* (April 2022); and then "The Many Taste Grooves of the Chang Family" landed in *Diabolical Plots* (May 2022)—to a bevy of glowing reviews. Her *Diabolical* story was even picked up for *LeVar Burton Reads* and made it onto the Locus Recommended Reading List. "Tina Yu and the Karaoke Time Machine" appeared in the January 2023 issue of *khōréō*.

Allison King's cousin is Lin King, who is also a writer and a translator. "We are still very close, and it's fun to have ended up both as professional writers. And a random fun fact is that an anagram of my name is 'Also Lin King,' which our parents did not intend!"

Allison King lives in Cambridge, "mostly because many of my friends have ended up here too, and there are amazing bookstores here." On her site, she describes herself as "a fullstack engineer building open-source tools to make information useful" whose work in technology "has ranged from semiconductors to platforms for community conversations to data privacy." When she's not working or writing, she is hanging out with her cat and dog, or drinking tea; in fact, she's planning to work a few hours a week in a local tea shop. "My current long-term goal is to be able to do a pull-up."

King's debut novel is *The Phoenix Pencil Company*, where "a hidden and nearly forgotten magic—of Reforging pencils, bringing the memories they contain back to life—holds the power to transform a young woman's relationship with her grandmother, and to mend long-lost connections across time and space." The book was released last month by HarperCollins imprint William Morrow.

Who do you see as your "writing heroes"—folks who inspired you or otherwise meant something to you; or, what are the works that you see as important to you, and why?

First would be Ruth Ozeki. I read *A Tale for the Time Being* in my Asian American Literature class in college and was so in awe of it. I bought her two previous books, *My Year of Meats* and *All Over Creation*, and also loved them. Ozeki is just so good at making the reader feel a full spectrum of emotions—her books are so funny yet also so sad at times, and always I learn something from them, either about the world or about myself. My book *The Phoenix Pencil Company* would not have existed if I had never read *A Tale for the Time Being* first. It was the first time I had read an Asian American experience portrayed so tenderly, especially its portrayal of intergenerational relationships.

Second would be Ken Liu. As a child, I was always very into fantasy books, but that dwindled a bit in college. It was not until I read Ken Liu's *The Paper Menagerie and Other Stories* that I feel like I entered my second phase of loving speculative fiction. It was certainly the first time I had read fantasy woven into Asian mythology/experiences, and it made me want to try my hand at it too. I also adored The Dandelion Dynasty series.

At what point did you decide to take writing seriously and to try to publish professionally?

Honestly, it was probably shortly after reading *The Grace of Kings*, the first in The Dandelion Dynasty series. I started writing epic fantasy, listening to podcasts, and from there learned about the SFF short story markets. I started submitting specifically to SFF markets in 2020. It wasn't really a decision, so much as I thought I'd give it a try, and then I couldn't stop.

You've sold a handful of short stories, and your novel just came out. What has your writer's journey been like so far? Has it been smooth, did things go the way you imagined they would?

My writer's journey started off a little bumpy but became really incredibly smooth later. I started off submitting short stories to the big literary places. I didn't really know what I was doing—I went to school for engineering, so I didn't know anything about query letters or how to submit short stories. It wasn't until I joined online SFF writing communities that I began to better understand how to go about submitting. The Dream Foundry Discord server, in particular, was so helpful in starting to understand the publishing industry and just how difficult it is to get a story published. Still, I'd write and submit, take it very personally every time I got a rejection, wallow for a while, then repeat.

When I got my first pro-rate acceptance from *Fantasy Magazine*, I was so thrilled. It is probably still one of my happiest memories—I remember running out of my room, telling my partner, and we just hugged and jumped around for a while. After that, I still got many rejections but developed a better intuition for the markets and what kind of stories they would like, and so had some more success that way.

In 2020, I shelved my epic fantasy and started working on what became *The Phoenix Pencil Company*. It started off as a short story (that also accumulated many rejections!) before I decided to make it into a novel. After my first draft, I submitted it to Reese's Book Club's LitUp fellowship and was accepted. In some ways, it felt like a golden ticket—the fellowship is really quite astounding, and made querying and going on sub go incredibly smoothly for me, thanks to the power of the Reese's Book Club brand.

Is there a relationship between your short fiction and your long fiction, whether in terms of themes, or skill sets and development, or anything else? Or do you see them as very separate, serving very different purposes?

There is definitely a relationship between my short and long fiction, mostly either in the exploration of technology or of memory. My most well-known short story is probably "The Many Taste Grooves of the Chang Family," first published in *Diabolical Plots*, then in audio on *LeVar Burton Reads*, and I see the themes of this story—a neutral piece of technology capable of evoking memories, a family caring for someone with Alzheimer's—to be direct predecessors to *The Phoenix Pencil Company*. I see "Taste Grooves" as a much smaller-scale version of *The Phoenix Pencil Company*, almost like a proof of concept.

The Phoenix Pencil Company also started off as a short story that never quite landed the way I wanted it to. The story was set solely in the 1940s at a pencil company in Shanghai. There wasn't enough room to get all the historical context in or to relate it back to the real world. For instance, there were these pencils that the family could make where they could bring the words they wrote back, and this proves dangerous in a time of war and government surveillance. But I had trouble making the story answer why this would matter to a reader today. It was not until I let it become a novel, that I added a parallel timeline set in the modern day about software and data privacy, that I felt the story worked.

What was the original inspiration for The Phoenix Pencil Company, and how did the story change or develop from the initial idea?

The instigator for the book was Helen Zia's *Last Boat Out of Shanghai: The Epic Story of the Chinese Who Fled Mao's Revolution*. It is an absolutely incredible nonfiction book that follows four families who left Shanghai in the 1940s/1950s. It made me start to wonder about my own family history, since my grandparents also left China for Taiwan at that time. The other inspiration is that my grandparents really did run a pencil company in China and then Taiwan. So, as I thought of my family history and the pencil company, this story was born.

As I said earlier, it started as a short story. But I felt very intimidated, knowing how much research I would have to do to write a book set in 1940s Shanghai. So when the short story wasn't working exactly, I expanded it to a novel and added a second timeline, set in modern-day Massachusetts, which is where I live now. I tried to give the second timeline as much familiarity with my real world as possible, as a way to counter how much work I knew I'd have to put in for the historical sections.

World War Two is a popular topic, explored by movies, books, comic books, and much more. What are your thoughts about why it remains popular, and what is distinctive about your approach or focus?

For me, I grew up with my grandparents, who did not exactly talk about the war, but it came up every so often. My grandfather had a scar on his arm from a bullet, and for a long time my family refused to buy Japanese cars (though eventually they caved and at one point we had three Toyotas). The war was something that had displaced them, so even if they did not talk about any details of the war, it colored so many of the things they did. For me, writing about the war was a way of trying to better understand what my grandparents may have lived through, and I think that is probably the case with a lot of other authors writing in the subgenre.

However, when I wrote the book, I was not trying to write a historical novel. I was even avoiding it, since I was sure I would get something wrong. I really wanted to tell a story about a family that made pencils in extraordinary times, and to explore the themes of who owns a story. My grandmother did not talk about the war, but she did talk about the pencil company. And I wanted to use the speculative elements to drive these themes home. The speculative element is purposefully neutral, though—it does give the main characters power, but not in a way that can change the tide of a war. So I think that is what is distinct in my approach—that there is a magical element, but a very contained one, that does not change the course of history but does highlight certain aspects of the war.

What were the challenges as well as the advantages of using epistolary storytelling?

The biggest challenge was seeing how much I could get away with explaining in a letter. In one timeline, Yun is recounting her own story to her cousin Meng, who lived with her through WWII and the Chinese Civil War. It was a challenge to relay to the reader the context of the war, while also hopefully not making the reader stop to wonder, "wait, why is she explaining this to her cousin who has also lived through this?" I think readers tend to give some leeway there, but that was definitely a balance to strike.

There were many advantages, though. For the same reason, I did not have to go into a ton of detail on historical settings. Where in a non-epistolary narrative, I might feel obligated to describe what their 1940s house looked like, in epistolary, that would feel quite out of place, to start describing your own house in a letter. I also think epistolary lets you home in on character and relationships in a way that is harder to do in other forms. In letters, it's all about your interactions with other people or settings, and your raw feelings regarding them. And guilt! Epistolary is a wonderful way to write a character's guilt.

The Library Journal review described the writing of The Phoenix Pencil Company, saying it "demonstrates a compelling voice in both literary historical fiction and technological stories . . . " In terms

of approach and craft, what do you see as crucial for developing a compelling voice?

This is another place where epistolary helps. There are two alternating points of view in *The Phoenix Pencil Company* that are both epistolary, so both are first person. They absolutely had to have different voices. There are little mechanics that were maybe cheat codes that helped me. For instance, in the modern day PoV, there are text messages and emojis. That all helps put me in the head of a teenager, and epistolary makes it easy to write all that teenage angst and embarrassment.

Voice is so hard though, and I'm definitely still learning. Sometimes, for me, it's a matter of getting my head into the voice, so I'll read books that are similar to the kind of voice I want my character to have. Yun's point of view, I was going for Elena Ferrante-esque, and Monica isn't too far off from Nao in *A Tale for the Time Being*. So if I ever felt like I lost the voice, I could pick up those books and reorient myself.

What are your favorite things about Yun and Monica as characters, and what were your favorite things about writing them?

I love that Yun lies a lot. She's the grandmother in Monica's chapters, so it felt really good to give her this un-grandmotherly characteristic in her own chapters. She's kind of a schemer, and though her lies sometimes get her in trouble, I think they also save her in some ways. She's a lifelong liar who is finally trying to write the truth of her story.

Monica was so much fun to write. Not so much Monica herself—she is quite straitlaced, shy, A+ student—but putting her in really awkward or embarrassing situations, especially if her grandmother instigated them. It was a delight to have Yun scheme against Monica, who she loves more than anything, but will also happily tease. But actually, I really admire Monica. I think people tend to be drawn to Yun's point of view because it is where all the action is. But I loved being able to write a quieter story alongside the WWII one, a story of a young woman not always getting it right, but absolutely trying her best.

What, for you, is the heart of this story, what is The Phoenix Pencil Company ultimately about?

It's ultimately about this love between a granddaughter and her grandmother, and how, even not knowing someone's whole story, we can still love them entirely.

What else do you have in the works that you'd like Clarkesworld readers to know about?

I am very slowly progressing on what will hopefully be my next novel. It's about the semiconductor industry, Taiwan, tea, and earthquakes. I'm learning a lot!

ABOUT THE AUTHOR

Arley Sorg is an associate agent at kt literary. He is a two-time World Fantasy Award Finalist and a two-time Locus Award Finalist for his work as co-Editor-in-Chief at *Fantasy Magazine*. Arley is also a SFWA Solstice Award Recipient, a Space Cowboy Award Recipient, and a finalist for two Ignyte Awards. Arley is senior editor at *Locus*, associate editor at both *Lightspeed* & *Nightmare*, a columnist for *The Magazine of Fantasy and Science Fiction* and an interviewer for *Clarkesworld*.

Diverse Bodies: A Conversation with Annalee Newitz

ARLEY SORG

Annalee Newitz was born in Santa Monica, CA, and grew up in Irvine. Their parents were both English teachers—their mother was from the south and began her teaching career in Watts; their dad taught at a community college. The family didn't have a television in their house, but they had a massive, two-story bookshelf that their dad had built. Their parents often took them to the library, where they explored science fiction. Newitz studied English at UC Berkeley (which included a few creative writing classes), where they also completed a PhD in English and American studies. They landed a job as a journalist after grad school, primarily focusing on technology and science.

Newitz has extensive experience in various kinds of journalism, including freelance and projects they started. They received a Knight Science Journalism Fellowship and worked as a research fellow at MIT; they were the culture editor for the *San Francisco Bay Guardian*; they were a policy analyst for the Electronic Frontier Foundation; they cofounded and ran SF website *io9*, which was eventually combined with *Gizmodo*; they worked for *Ars Technica* as tech culture editor; then they became a contributor to *The New York Times* op-ed section, up until 2023. They are a columnist for *New Scientist* magazine, and they cohost *Our Opinions Are Correct* with Charlie Jane Anders, a multi-Hugo-winning podcast Newitz and Anders launched in 2018.

Annalee Newitz is also a well-respected nonfiction author. Their dissertation was published as *Pretend We're Dead: Capitalist Monsters in American Pop Culture* in 2006; *Scatter, Adapt, and Remember: How Humans Will Survive a Mass Extinction* came out in 2013—and was nominated for the LA Times Book Prize in science—*Four Lost Cities: A Secret History of the Urban Age* was published in 2021; and *Stories Are Weapons: Psychological Warfare and the American Mind* in 2024.

Newitz hit the fiction scene in 2010 with short story "The Gravity Fetishist," which appeared in a magazine called *Flurb*, edited by Rudy Rucker. "Twilight of the Eco-Terrorist" came out in the May 2011 *Apex*, and in 2014, they had pieces in *Lightspeed*, *Shimmer*, and more, beginning a steady career as a fiction writer. Short story "When Robot and Crow Saved East St. Louis" (*Slate* Dec 2018) was a Sturgeon Award winner, and "A Hole in the Light" (*Sunday Morning Transport* Oct 2022) was a Sturgeon Award finalist.

Debut novel *Autonomous* (Tor 2017) was published to critical acclaim. It was also a finalist for Campbell Memorial, Nebula, and Locus awards, and won a Lambda Award. *The Future of Another Timeline* (Tor 2019) also enjoyed critical praise, such as starred reviews and being a PW Pick, as well as being a finalist for a Dragon Award, a Locus Award, and winning a Sidewise Award. Similarly, *The Terraformers* (Tor 2023) was well-received, earning glowing and starred reviews, as well as being a Nebula and Locus awards finalist.

Annalee Newitz splits time between San Francisco, where they have lived for a while, and Vancouver, Canada. "What keeps me coming back to San Francisco is partly its beauty and culture—and by 'culture' I mean the indie arts and music scene, but also indie tech and science—and partly the fact that it has been my home for so long. When I was a kid, I always wanted to live in San Francisco, and I wound up spending my adult life here. So it feels more like home than anywhere else."

They hope to visit as many labs as possible, and they have a bucket list of labs. "One of the great things about being a science journalist is that I have an excellent reason to tour all kinds of labs. I think the most amazing labs I have ever visited are the Wave Lab at Oregon State

University at Corvallis, and the archaeological excavation at Çatalhöyük in Turkey. This summer I'm going to visit two archaeological sites—Knossos on Crete, and Tharros on Sardinia—as I start research on my next science book, which is a history of parties in the ancient world."

Their novella *Automatic Noodle* is scheduled for publication next month with Tordotcom, and has already received starred reviews from *Publishers Weekly*, *Library Journal*, and *Booklist*. They are also working on a science book for WW Norton called *Celebration: An Ancient History of Parties*, and a novel for Tor, tentatively called *A Wall is Also a Road*, which is a romance about a graduate student who is a slime mold from beyond the galaxy.

You worked as a journalist for quite a while. In terms of craft, process, or anything else, is there some kind of interplay, connection, or influence between journalism and fiction writing for you?

At this point, they are completely intertwined. In fact, I was just saying to my editor, Stephanie Stein at Tor, that she should get ready for my next novel to be full of all the ancient civilizations that I'm writing about in my next nonfiction book. Of course, I always heavily fictionalize and transform my journalism when I incorporate it into fiction. I suspect there are a lot of details that nobody but me would notice. I also feel like learning to write novels has dramatically improved my nonfiction books. I've learned how to craft a narrative arc, how to balance description with dialogue, and how to build a world that the reader can believe in. One of the unsung skills of science journalism is worldbuilding—sometimes you get a concept that's very difficult to explain, and you have to paint a picture for readers so that they understand things like the shape of the galaxy or the way ancient people built their houses. Fiction gives us the tools to do that, while nonfiction gives us the ability to incorporate evidence from real life.

Automatic Noodle is your upcoming novella, and you have published a lot of work besides novels. Do you feel that anything notable has changed about your writing since you drafted your debut novel, Autonomous?

I'm a lot more confident now, when it comes to starting a novel. I think one of the things I had to unlearn as I transitioned from journalism to fiction was that I can just make things happen in a story because I want them to. Obviously, in journalism, you report what has actually happened, and if you write about something that didn't happen, you're in a lot of trouble. I had a really hard time letting go of the desire to make my fiction work sort of like journalism. Of course, I was making everything up, but I would get anxious when it felt too much like I was grabbing the wheel and forcing events to occur.

Now I'm a lot more comfortable making my characters do things and justifying it however I want. I mean, I'm very committed to emotional realism and plausibility. But I'm less afraid to just get weird and allow, for example, a train to fall in love with a cat. The other thing that's really changed for me is my appreciation for building characters. I used to not think about building up a character—I would just sort of channel this other person and not think too hard about why they were doing what they did. Now, I spend more time thinking about the entire arc of a character's experiences and choices. Maybe that feels less magical in some ways, but it's so much better for the story itself.

There was a lot of buzz around your last nonfiction book, Stories Are Weapons. In your PEN Ten interview, you talked about stories in terms of "psychological infrastructure," saying, "psychological infrastructure is a lot more fungible than urban infrastructure—reading a new kind of story can be life-changing." Is there any connection or relationship between Stories Are Weapons and Automatic Noodle?

There's a whole subplot in *Automatic Noodle* about robophobic propaganda online, which was heavily influenced by the research I'd done. One of the main characters is a "stay behind" soldier, trained to remain alert for US-backed terrorists and counterrevolutionary forces in California. I think the interviews I did with psyops practitioners and experts for *Stories Are Weapons* really shaped that character. Of course, I had always known about wartime trauma, but writing *Stories Are Weapons* made me realize that propaganda leaves a lasting scar on survivors of violence. People sometimes want to argue that psyops are harmless because nobody is blown up, but that's just not true. Many people have been deeply traumatized by intentionally brutal political messages and media manipulation, and they will be carrying that hurt for the rest of their lives.

Autonomous came out in 2017. If you think on your three novels as a progression of interests and storytelling approaches, what does

that journey look like, and how does Automatic Noodle speak to that journey?

I feel like every novel is full of mistakes that I've tried to correct with the next book. But then I make new mistakes! I guess that's the messy joy of the creative process. With *Automatic Noodle*, I finally felt like I was writing a book where I loved every single character. I didn't feel ambivalent about them. And that really felt good.

Automatic Noodle features "a crew of leftover robots." Literature, TV, and film, time and again, come back to robots. What do you see as the cause of the enduring appeal of stories about robots, what is the appeal for you personally, and what do you see as most interesting about your approach to robots in this book?

Self-aware, autonomous robots are mythical creatures based on the promises of technology, but currently, they are more mythical than real. So I think their appeal is probably similar to many other mythical figures like the vampire or the dragon. They are part of a shared story we tell about ourselves, and we can project many things onto them. Somebody like Elon Musk imagines that robots will be the perfect happy slaves. For me, robots are a way to explore queer identity—specifically, what it's like when your body and your feelings in that body don't match social demands. Sometimes a robot is a person, but they look like an octopus, or they have a body that's huge and burly, but they feel soft and cozy. The robots in my novels are generally trying to figure out their genders and desires in a world that doesn't acknowledge them as people—and doesn't understand how they might experience sexual desire.

Honestly, I often feel like I'm trying to rescue my own body from all the demands and expectations placed on it by my culture. As a nonbinary person, I don't often present as a gender that is easily understood. But also, I grew up hearing that I was supposed to enjoy very specific kinds of sex—like, everyone is supposed to feel the same kinds of pleasure in the same places on their bodies. That's not true, though. Sexual pleasure is as diverse as people are. I love going on a journey of bodily discovery with my robots, as they figure out what gives them joy, and who they want to love, and what makes them horny. Even better, they can reconfigure their bodies in ways that humans can't – so there's definitely some wish fulfillment in there too. One of my robot characters, Sweetie, gets the world's easiest and most delightful top surgery ever. Definitely a lot easier than the eight weeks of recovery when I got top surgery! Plus, I didn't get to install a twinkling LED wire in my scar. So yeah. A little wish fulfillment for sure.

The book imagines a future where California has split off from the United States, various rights for robots, and more. What are a few of your favorite science-fictional tidbits from the book that you see as plausible, and what are a few of your favorites that are just fun imaginings?

I do think it's plausible that the United States will break up, probably sooner rather than later. And if that happened, I also wouldn't be surprised if the remaining rump of the US became a haven for crypto scams, like in the book. The fun imaginings in the book are all related to the robots. Maybe one day we will have robots who are people like humans, but I don't think that will happen for a long time—certainly not by the 2050s. That said, if robots ever do become people, I guarantee there will be robophobes who want to deprive them of rights. Another thing I really enjoyed imagining for the book is a piece of worldbuilding about the California government, which is that Miwoks and other Indigenous nations have become very powerful in California after the war. The Salesforce Tower has been renamed Klamath Tower, which is both symbolically important but also my way of alerting readers that this is a city where the land's original peoples are once again in control of major pieces of real estate.

What was the original inspiration for this book, and how did the story transform or change over drafts and edits?

I was absolutely inspired by my love of biang biang noodles and watching tons of videos about how to make them. (No, I did not ever learn to make biang biang noodles, but I did discover many wonderful places to buy them from people who know what they're doing.) Also, because we are in a time of horrific wars and traumatic propaganda, I wanted to write about recovery and repair from violence. The main way the story changed as I edited was that I added a LOT more detail about the noodles and the bots' relationship with them. Many thanks go to food writers/creators Esther Tseng, Kristie Hang, Michi Trota, and Meghan McCarron, all of whom read early drafts of the novella and talked to me about restaurant culture, cooking, and debates over "authentic" ethnic food.

What can you tell us about the central characters of Automatic Noodle? How would you describe them, and what are the things that challenge them the most in the narrative?

This is my first ensemble cast book! The action centers on a group of restaurant workers—four are California bots and one is an undocumented human refugee from America. The four bots are Staybehind (he/him), a humanoid military bot recovering from wartime trauma, who discovers a love of interior decorating; Sweetie (she/her), a three-legged wheeled bot who learns to love her body through radical reengineering; Hands (they/them), a bot who is nothing but two arms and a torso, who yearns to make perfect noodles with their exquisitely calibrated hands; and Cayenne (they/them), a soft octopus bot who has taste sensors on each arm and does flavor maxxing to earn coin. Robles is their human friend, who can help them navigate a world where bots are still second-class citizens, at best. Together, they have to figure out how to trust each other, run a restaurant, and navigate all the red tape in San Francisco that restricts business ownership to humans.

As your first ensemble cast book, was it tricky to manage a range of perspectives—did you have specific tools or techniques you used?

It was very tricky, and I tried a lot of different things before settling on the structure I have now. At first, I thought each chapter would be strictly from one character's point of view, and that I would switch between them round-robin style. That turned out to be incredibly artificial and clunky. So then I just let their perspectives flow into each other as if all of them were telling a story to a friend and they were kind of interrupting each other and offering their perspective, and then another character would come in and say, "But hey, this is what I saw."

So most of the time, each chapter is devoted to one character, but not always. In some chapters, it starts out from one character's point of view and blends into the next character's point of view. It's all in close third person, though, so I think it's usually pretty obvious whose perspective we're seeing things from. Or, at least I hope so. Honestly, it was much easier than my second novel, *The Future of Another Timeline*, where I had two characters who were both speaking in the first person. Why the hell did I do that? Never again.

What is this book ultimately about for you—what is the heart of the story?

It's about recovering from historical trauma. Right now, we're all being traumatized by war, corporate cruelty, and environmental destruction. I wanted to imagine what happens after war, as people recover and repair their environment.

Is there anything else you'd like to share with Clarkesworld readers about Automatic Noodle, you, your work, or your upcoming projects?

I do want to give a shout-out to an anthology that I edited with Karen Lord and Malka Older, which is coming out from Saga Press in December. It's called *We Will Rise Again*, and it's a collection of short stories, essays, and interviews about protest and resistance. There are some incredible original stories in there, which explore everything from magical war and futuristic online propaganda to restorative justice and protest art. It's just an incredible collection, and I'm really proud of it. Plus, working with Karen and Malka was a dream. I'm a huge fan of both their work, and I think people are really going to love the collection of stories we put together.

ABOUT THE AUTHOR

Arley Sorg is an associate agent at kt literary. He is a two-time World Fantasy Award Finalist and a two-time Locus Award Finalist for his work as co-Editor-in-Chief at *Fantasy Magazine*. Arley is also a SFWA Solstice Award Recipient, a Space Cowboy Award Recipient, and a finalist for two Ignyte Awards. Arley is senior editor at *Locus*, associate editor at both *Lightspeed* & *Nightmare*, a columnist for *The Magazine of Fantasy and Science Fiction* and an interviewer for *Clarkesworld.*

Editor's Desk: Taking a Moment to Smell the Roses

NEIL CLARKE

July is our annual anniversary, but not the one celebrating our first issue. Nineteen years ago, while attending Readercon, Sean Wallace and I had a discussion about the state of short fiction that led to creation of this magazine. Prior to that, I had no plans to enter publishing. Six years later, also at Readercon, a heart attack nearly ended my life. Among the many side-effects of that brush with death was the realization that I had stumbled into a career I loved and needed to leave my old one behind. It took some time, but I eventually did. (Amusingly, in a weird twist of maintaining some sort of cosmic balance, Sean seems to have drifted more into my old line of work.) Nineteen years after the start of this journey, we're returning to the scene of the crime. For the first time in years, Readercon will be held at the hotel where all those events occurred.

Behind our tables in the dealer's room, we'll likely continue our nineteen-year discussion about the state of short fiction. I can't say whether or not there will be anything life-changing, but I now know better than to rule it out. We've had fantastic seats from which to watch the big changes in our field and even made some marks of our own. I doubt that either one of us anticipated that we'd still be doing this nearly two decades later, but here we are. Older and perhaps creakier, but still enjoying the ride.

This year, we have some celebrating to do. Several of our stories have been on the receiving end of a lot of award attention this year. Isabel J. Kim's story "Why Don't We Just Kill the Kid In the Omelas Hole" has won the BSFA, Nebula, and Locus Awards. A. W. Prihandita's novelette "Negative Scholarship on the Fifth State of Being" won a Nebula Award.

Octavia Cade's article "Fact, Fiction, and Feeling: Ecological Grief in a Changing World" won a Sir Julius Vogel Award.

And then there are all the stories that have been nominated for awards yet to be announced!

Finalists for the Theodore Sturgeon Memorial Award:

- "Swarm X1048 – Ethological Field Report: Canis Lupus Familiaris, '6'" by F.E. Choe
- "Hello! Hello! Hello!" by Fiona Jones
- "Why Don't We Just Kill the Kid In the Omelas Hole" by Isabel J. Kim

Finalists for the Hugo Awards:

- "Why Don't We Just Kill the Kid In the Omelas Hole" by Isabel J. Kim
- "The Brotherhood of Montague St. Video" by Thomas Ha

Finalists for the Ignyte Awards:

- "Fractal Karma" by Arula Ratnakar
- "Negative Scholarship on the Fifth State of Being" by A. W. Prihandita

Finalist for the Aurora Award:

- "A World of Milk and Promises" by R H Wesley

Finalist for the Eugie Foster Memorial Award for Short Fiction

- "Negative Scholarship on the Fifth State of Being" by A. W. Prihandita

The winners of those awards will be announced in the weeks ahead, but win or lose, they've made a mark.

When it comes to the awards, I'm quite proud of the accomplishments of our authors. It's always been about the stories for us, so seeing them recognized in this way, or even with just a few kind words by a fan, means a lot to us. We're accustomed to them being in the forefront–where they should be–but every now and then the light shines over on us too. I'm a Hugo finalist for Best Editor Short Form this year and just won the Locus Award for Best Editor. It's very flattering to receive that kind of attention and after the last few years, a well-timed pat on the back when I needed it the most.

This year, however, we have something entirely new to add to our list. *Clarkesworld* has received the Locus Award for Best Magazine.

This is our first time winning in that category and it's one of the few awards that a professional genre magazine can receive. There are no names on this award, just *Clarkesworld.* I like that. It's all of us as one. The authors, artists, translators, slush readers, proofreaders, interviewer, narrator, and editors. So congratulations to the *Clarkesworld* class of 2024! I couldn't be working with a better group of people and it's an honor to share this honor with all of you.

And, of course, a thank you is owed to all our readers for their support and kind words in the past year. These awards are a reflection of your appreciation and that means so much. As you know from my editorials, this is a tough field to work in. It's people like you that make it all the more worthwhile.

Now it's back to work. I have a convention to pack for. Hopefully we'll see a few of you there!

ABOUT THE AUTHOR

Neil Clarke is the editor of *Clarkesworld Magazine, Forever Magazine,* and several anthologies, including the Best Science Fiction of the Year series. He is a three-time winner of the Hugo Award for Best Editor Short Form, two-time winner of the Locus Award for Best Editor, a four-time winner of the Chesley Award for Best Art Director, and a recipient of the Kate Wilhelm Solstice Award. His next anthology, *Best Science Fiction of the Year: Volume 8*, was published by Night Shade Books in September. He currently lives in NJ with his wife and two sons.

Alone

COVER ART BY MATT DIXON

ABOUT THE ARTIST

Matt Dixon is a freelance illustrator and concept artist from the UK. He paints digitally, a medium which first captured his imagination when he began to assemble images from ASCII characters on a Commodore VIC-20 more than forty years ago.

Matt first contributed art to a videogame in 1988 and continues to work for clients in the games industry. Alongside client projects, Matt is the creator of the "Transmissions" of robot art, a personal project started in 2005 to explore feelings and emotions that might be difficult to express in other ways, while indulging his fondness for painting rusty automata.

His favorite color is green.

Printed in Dunstable, United Kingdom

65098662R00088